Norview

"Got some shit going on that I'd Rather not say...Know some niggas dead and gone that won't see another day...Know its niggas out here snitching but they'll smile in your face...Ask the lord for protection every time I lay and pray," I sung along to 'Korb Skii's' 'Cool Young Nigga' as my boyfriend Rod and I cruised to our destination in our newly copped Black, Infiniti m45.

"Dang Candy. I'm tired of driving," said Rod as he turned down the music using a switch on the steering wheel.

"Too bad. You the one with the license," I replied as I reclined back in my seat. "If I crash this whip are you gonna pay for another one?"

"What?" asked Rod, face screwed up. "I'm not trying hear that shit. You drive anytime you want to. You just don't feel like it right now. I'm not stupid."

"Well at least you know me," I followed.

So, me and my nigga was on our way to meet our new plug, that's a drug connect for anyone who doesn't know. But yeah, this was like a dream come true for us. At least for me. Just last month I was locked up, mad as hell sitting in a cold ass cell. I was a booster, I could steal your shoes off your feet while you were tying them on, easily. And before you go judging me let me at least say that I never really even liked to steal, but shit, I hated being broke even more. But when I viewed my pretty ass face plastered all over the evening news, caught red handed walking out of MacArthur Mall with thousands of dollars' worth of merchandise, I knew it was time to find a new profession.

I'll be damned if I stay up all night writing papers and studying, I can't do hair, I'm not wiping some old wrinkled lady's ass and I definitely aint taking no orders at Mickey d's. Drugs was my only option. I'd been around the shit my whole life. All my uncles and cousins used and sold and so did almost every one of my Mom's many boyfriends. And it didn't take long at all to figure out what I should invest in. Without question, Weed and not just any ol weed, I'm talking Gas, loud, fruit, pressure, high quality smoke was the most popular pass time in Virginia. Shit, probably the whole world. Everybody I knew smoked it. I was actually kinda mad I hadn't thought of it earlier. This was a sure fire way to get my bands up. And with my boo just so happening to get his school refund check, everything fell in line. Made one phone call and it was on and popping.

It didn't take long at all to progress. Like I said, everyone in Town knew me. And after being one of the top boosters in the city I already knew what it took to rise to the top. Consistency. Consistency was the key to success. With consistency and great product we couldn't lose. In no time me and Rod had risen to great heights. Selling weed became our life. We ate, slept and breathed it. From the moment we opened our eyes till the second we shut them our phones were booming. It got to the point, we even had to cut our phones off at night. Even then niggas was knocking at our door. I know, I know, they say never hustle where you sleep. But shit, we don't just sell the weed, we smoke the shit too and we all know weed gives you that lazy feeling. There was no way I was getting up, taking niggas weed all day. I mean if it was some real money, yeah. But dimes and dubs hell no, you gotta come to me. Plus, won't no nigga stupid enough to try anything.

But like I was saying, this whole weed thing was really working out. Guess it's safe to say we were on our way to being hood rich. What's hood rich, one might ask? Let me explain. Hood rich aint really rich. You can't buy a house or retire in Miami or nothing like that. But what you could do is anything a street nigga or street bitch like myself wants to do. Including, copping all the latest clothes and shoes, V.I.P. in the club, jewelry and trips. Trips is what I'm most excited about. Me and Rod want to go to Atlanta next weekend. Neither of us have ever been. That's why meeting this new plug was essential. I don't even know the nigga, never seen him a day in my life but a real good friend of mine put me on to him. His prices are unbelievable and I was told he always has some killer on deck. This could put me and Rod right where we need be. At the top where we belonged.

We pulled up around back at the Motel Six. The Plug had told us to park there and he'd walk over to us.

"You know you gotta do all the talking right," I told Rod as he backed in between two cars.

"Why? You know I hate talking," Rod complained.

"First of all stop whinin like a lil' bitch. 'Why I gotta talk'" I said mocking Rod in a childish tone.

"Forget you. I don't sound like that," Rod replied calmly.

"Boy, yes you do. You needa start just doin what the hell I say," I said, unbuckling my seat beat.

"Hold on. Who do you think you're talking to, first of all? You gonna quit acting like you the man. I'm the man around here, don't forget," Rod said unsuccessfully attempting to take charge.

"Well I can't tell. You complainin bout talkin to the nigga like you scared or somethin."

"Scared? When did anybody say anything about being scared? I'm just not big on talking. There's nothing wrong with that," Rod explained.

"Yes it is when we tryna do business. How's it gonna look if a female doin all the talkin. I'm tryna help you. You the one who's gonna be embarrassin yourself. Not me."

Rod sat speechless shaking his head.

I can't lie, Rod is my baby, shit I may even love the nigga. Actually I'm pretty sure I do. Never told him or anything. I'm not with all the lovey dovey bullshit. But yeah, I love the nigga. Found that out the very first time we ever had some bomb ass sex. No, it wasn't the fact that he savagely fulfilled my sexual desires. Of course that was a plus. But it was the fact that I could actually enjoy lying in bed with him afterwards. To me that was big. Usually after sex I'm outta there ASAP and if we're at my crib, soon as the nigga get to snoring I wake that ass up. Aint no cuddling. Still, whether I love the nigga or not. There was no denying that he wasn't my usual type. Don't get me wrong. Rod was fine. Tall, athletically built, nice size dick, knew how to work it, good teeth and he had the most gorgeous light caramel skin. And I can't forget about his hair. The nigga shit was Red. After all these years of fucking with these ol everyday looking ass niggas I'd finally found me an exotic one. Only thing was, Rod wasn't from Norview, he wasn't even from Virginia. He was from a remote, far away land. Ok, maybe I'm exaggerating but he was from Oklahoma. I didn't even know they had black people there. And judging from the way he walked, talked and carried himself I wouldn't be surprised if he was in fact the only nigga there. I can't even lie though, sometimes that white boy shit he be on pisses me the hell off, still, most of the time it intrigued me. I liked it. He was different, pure. At times I even felt like I was corrupting him. But fuck it, the way I see it I'm doing him a favor. I'm showing him a world he's never seen and I'm giving it to him raw.

We sat in silence for a second before my phone rung. Looked at the caller I.D. and it was him. We'd been texting already.

"Hea," I said handing the phone over to Rod.

He breathed heavily before answering. "Hello."

"Yo whatsup bro. Is that you sittin over there in the black M45?" the strong voice over the speaker phone asked, as Rod and I both looked around for him.

"Yeah its me."

"Bet I'm about to walk over."

"Cool."

"Was that so hard?" I asked as Rod hung up the phone. He ignored me as I finally spotted the guy walking up. Tall, brown skin, low cut, nothing special. He'd parked a couple rows over. "There he is right there," I said looking to my left as he carefully eyeballed the entire parking lot while strolling over in gear that screamed anything but 'I have money'. That's common though. The niggas with the most money be looking the bummiest. Can't say all of them, because some dumbass niggas love stunting, flashy jewelry, designer clothes, making sure everybody and they Mama knew they was balling. Sad to say, I'm probably one of the flashy ones. I can't help it though. I come from a long line of show-offs. No matter how broke we were, everybody in town knew that my family was gonna have the latest fashion. Dressing fly was like a bill where I was from. And not some little cell phone bill or anything like that. I'm talking Rent, Car note type of bill. To be completely honest Rent and car note would sometimes get delayed if some new Jordan's were released. Some might say that's stupid. But like the old saying goes, 'You gotta dress to impress'. Not that I gotta impress anyone but it's definitely a must I remind you that I'm better than you each and every time you glance over to me. Don't blame me though, blame my mother and nine times out ten she's gonna tell you, don't blame her, blame her mama. So, like I said, it runs in my family. It's in my blood, it's a 'Parker' thing.

He hopped in. Instantly the odor of Grade A marijuana surrounded my nose. He slapped Rod five. "Whatsup my G. I'm Don."

"I'm Rod," replied Rod, shyly.

"Whatsup Lil Mama," said Don directed to me.

I smirked. Fuck wrong with him calling me Lil Mama? I'm gonna be bigger than him some day. Aint shit little about me except maybe this little deuce deuce stashed in my purse. I had a purse for every outfit I rocked and I always made sure each bag was large enough for my pistol.

"Yeah man I 'ma keep it short. I got the best gas you gon find. I usually have round two, three flavors at a time," spat Don smoothly. "Sour diesel, cookies, Candy Kush, all that shit. I heard through the grape vine, you be runnin through the packs daily, getting money."

"Yeah, something like that." Replied Rod.

"Bet. If that's true we gon do some real good business. The more you come through I might start hittin yall with more and more shit. I just gotta know I can trust you."

"True," said Rod as he nodded his head.

"Bet. Well all I got today is the sour, you can kill the game with this. Straight Gas. Real deal shit. Shits so potent, makes your whole mouth numb. "

"Cool," Rod said handing Don the money as he pulled out a gigantic zip lock bag full of lime green smoke from inside the crotch area of his jeans before slickly sliding it up to Rod.

"I swear to God they gonna love that shit," said Don, enthused.

"Word," followed Rod as he looked over the product.

"Bet. Hit me up," He said slapping fives once again.

"No doubt," replied Rod.

"This can be the start of somethin epic. Keep rockin with me and yall can take over Norview in no time," he said as he exited the whip.

"Damn that shit is funky," I said as he stepped out.

"Hell yeah," said Rod as he looked over the product.

Despite the fact we'd spent our last dollar on the smoke, something told me this was going to be a great day. With an entire town of eager teens and young adults awaiting the arrival of our new shipment, my purse was sure to swell up in no time. I looked over to my baby, he'd let the sunroof back and the suns piercing glow shot down on him and at that moment I realized just how perfect he was. As I struggled to figure out which were deeper, his red, 360 waves or the round dimples that peeked out from his cheeks, he glanced over to me smiling, revealing his gloss white teeth. I thought to myself, I'm one lucky girl.

Naw actually, forget that, he's the lucky one. Yeah Rod's fine and all but I'm no slouch either. From a scale of 1-10 I'd have to give myself a 10, shit maybe even higher. And I aint one of those ugly ass bitches who say shit like that to try to boost my already low self-esteem. No, I'm talking straight facts. And no I'm not basing my opinion on Facebook or Instagram likes. Sure, some dumb ignorant dick in the booty ass niggas might say I'm too dark but any real man with taste knows I'm top of the line. I can count on one hand how many times in my life I've worn makeup and my chocolate complexion still appears smooth and clear as the day the Dr. smacked me on the Ass. My eyes, wide, full of life, lips and nose of an Egyptian Goddess. Titties, aren't huge but their firm and perky, flat stomach, slim waist and Ass for days. Maybe not days but certainly hours. Ok, ok, I'm still lying, I don't have a big ol butt, but don't get it fucked up I aint got no pancake back there. Plus when I bend this thing over, best believe it shakes like a sinner on judgement day. If that aint the description of a bad bitch, than I don't know what to tell you. Well actually I do, Fuck you. I'm the shit and I'm going to be even better once I really run my money up. Not because I need to purchase expensive clothes to make myself look better, I was blessed with an undeniable since of style. I can kill in an outfit designed by Louis Vuitton or a $20 fit from the local thrift store. What I need money for is simply the extra confidence. There's nothing like walking past a group of broke bitches and knowing that you possess the power to buy their whole life if you pleased. With that being said I shot out a mass text to all of our plucks, it was time to get this show on the road. But first we needed to stop past the crib.

"We about to kill em today baby. I can just feel it. My palms itchin," I said as I rubbed my left palm with my right hands finger tips.

"Maybe you should start washing your hands," followed Rod as he continued driving, focusing on the road.

I burst out laughing. "Nigga Shut up."

"What? You're the one talking about your hands itching. If something itches, 9 times out 10 its dirty, wash em."

"Hold on. Are you serious?"

"Serious about what? Your dirty palms?"

"Are you tellin me you've never heard anyone say that their palms were itchin?"

"Can't say that I have. Is it one of your 'black' sayings that I don't know anything about?" Rod asked as he held up imaginary quotations with his fingers.

"Uh yeah. I can't believe you," I said shaking my head. "When someone says their palms are itchin it simply means they're about to get some money."

"Really? Who made that up?"

"Nigga, I don't know who made it up. It's just somethin everybody knows. What the hell do they teach yall in Oklahoma?"

"This," said Rod as he grabbed my left breast.

"Boy, you better stop," I said before licking my lips seductively. "You don't even know what to do with one of them."

"Yeah right. I can show you better than I can tell you."

"Show, deez nutz," I said jokingly as Rod parked the whip in front of our Apartment complex.

We made our way out of the vehicle. I lived on Ivaloo St. one of the most poppin street in all of Norview. The Loo, is what we called it. Been here all my life. Back in the day, it was just your everyday hood. Couple fights here in there, couple hustlers and feigns on the block but for the most part things were peaceful, we were like one big happy family. Honestly, the entire Norview was like that.

See, Norviews a small town but it was the perfect mixture of black and white. We live in Virginia, I guess you can consider that the South but as far as racism was concerned, I never even noticed it. Not saying it didn't exist but I guess it just wasn't blatant. Well at least, until a couple years ago. A white cop got murdered by a black guy and after that all hell broke loose. Murders, robberies, anything negative was an everyday thing. A gang was even formed, 'The Warriors' and suddenly everybody was a so called 'savage'. Guys I'd been going to school with since I was 5 suddenly transformed into super thugs. Niggas was dropping out school left and right. Bitches, getting pregnant .

Unfortunately, I fell victim to both. Got pregnant at 15 and dropped out the same day I found out. I don't know, I guess I thought I was grown or something. That's when I was fucking with Chop. He was a Warrior. Certified gangster. That shit used to turn me on. He just had this persona that was mouthwatering. And the nigga won't even cute. In fact he was quite ugly, kinda looked like a gorilla, big ol oversized nose that matched his big ol jumbo lips, actually mostly everything on him was oversized, minus the dick.

But I swear he was the ugliest pretty nigga you'd ever meet, if that makes any since. Fresh cut, new outfits damn near every day, and he was so laid back and smooth, exuding confidence, scented swag shot out his pours and leaked all over his body. He was the shit and as far as the streets go he was my professor.

And I wasn't his only student. Everyone around looked up to him. Natural Born Leader, with a Mike Tyson knockout blow, a snipers aim and the hustle of Big Meech. I'd already grown up around it but he gave me a front row seat onto 'A

Gangster's Life'. Too bad, that wasn't the only thing he taught me. I also learned how to take a hit.

Chop wasn't all bad but like a lot of niggas out here he believed that if he felt disrespected in any way, violence was the only remedy. He even explained it in a way that my dumbass agreed with him. I thought couples were supposed to fight. And the crazy thing about it is, I would've probably still been with the nigga today, but his ass fucked around and up left me. Yep, found some school girl and moved in with the bitch. And that's not even the end, I was still fucking with his nothing ass. I went from being the main bitch to the side, like a fool. And would've still been there till this day if he wouldn't't've gotten her pregnant. I had no choice but to leave then, everyone in town was already calling me stupid.

Over the couple years I'd dealt with him I'd already fought and lost all my closest girlfriends, either they'd fucked him or I thought they were trying too. With no one to talk too, I was lost, without a clue as of who I was. With nothing to live for I'd sunk down so low that suicide was the only other option. Luckily I'm too strong for that, so with every ounce of strength I had in me I left him in the past.

Lord knows it wasn't easy, probably the toughest thing I've ever had to do. For months I dreamed about him nightly, fantasizing about the day he'd change. But as I heard rumors of him putting his new girl through everything he'd already put me through, I slowly came to the realization that there probably wasn't any

changing for him. Still, can't say I regret a second, I wouldn't be the strong woman

that I am today without him. So yeah I was a dumb bitch. But on my Mama that

was the first and last time. That's why I'm so hard on Rod. I have to be in control.

Aint no way I'm playing the fool again. Fuck that.

"Whatsup. Whatsup," I greeted Nhi, who was standing outside my apartment

door, draped in all the latest designer gear, smoking a cigarette.

We stayed in a four family unit, Nhi and his family were one of our upstairs

neighbors. He was only about 14 or 15, I guess he calls himself being a 'Warrior'

too. But too be honest that shit wasn't even the same as it used to be. Most of the

older niggas who started it were locked up and niggas like Chop were all about

themselves. They could care less about the little niggas. Unless of course they

needed them to do something stupid or dangerous, then they'd pay them a few

dollars or sometimes even make them do it for free.

"Whatsup Candy. What's good Rod?" he replied in his best gangster

impersonation. Ok maybe he wasn't impersonating but I knew the boy since he

was five all this thug shit is just funny to me.

We both spoke back.

"Yo," he said looking around before continuing to speak as if he had something top notch to say. "Whatever yall got is funky as a bitch. I gotta cop some of that," he said as he sniffed into the air.

"No doubt," I said as Rod and I stopped to converse. "Yeah this that rapper weed. You aint smoked nothin like this before," I said looking down to my purse, where I had stashed the weed.

"Yep," Rod co-signed. Of course we hadn't smoked it yet. It could be some straight

t trash that just smelled like good weed, still we had to promote it like it was the best in town.

"Hell yeah! Rapper weed?" he shouted excitedly. "Soon as I hit my swipe lick I'm gonna hit yall up Asap I need that!"

"Bet," I said before I thought about it. "Matter fact I'm gonna give you a free sack in a second."

"Foreal?" Nhi shouted, excitedly. "I swear yall the best weed dealers in the world. I'm still gonna pay yall back tomorrow. Gotta lotta money coming in later."

Like a lot of people in Norview, Nhi was a swiper. Yeah, you still had your classic hustlers like Rod and I. But for the most part we were few and far between.

I can't really blame them though. Who wants to hustle all day when you can scam

the bank or major department stores out of money? A lot of hustlers hate on them

and say their taking the easy way out. I don't know about all that. To be

completely honest, I really have no idea just what the fuck swipers even do. Just

like most people, all I know is they post those statuses on Instagram and Facebook

saying shit like 'If you want to make $200 like my status'. Initially when I first

started seeing people post stuff like that I thought they were lying but as I started to

see more and more people uploading selfies holding thousands of dollars in cash I

knew it was real. Still, I never indulged, Chop always told me you get way more

time for fucking with the White Man's money then hustling and I damn sure aint

trying to do a lot of time. Instead, I'll just enjoy the benefits of having swiper

customers. They're the best. They spend money like it's going out of style.

"You're good bro, you don't have to pay us back," replied Rod, declining his

offer. "Just be careful doing whatever you're doing."

"Yep". I followed. "You like a lil' bro, don't wanna see you get jammed

up."

"Thanks yall," he said taking a drag from his cigarette. "No doubt."

"No problem. We'll be right back," replied Rod as we walked into the

hallway of our apartment complex.

May not seem like it but honestly, even though Nhi may not have needed the free weed, I still feel as though I had done a good deed. Candy love the kids. I can relate to them, it wasn't too long ago I was in their position. I'm happy I'm able to supply them smoke for free or cheaper prices. It aint like I'm selling them crack. Weed is natural, it's from the earth. It's legal all across the country. I even started smoking weed around Nhi's age. Aint like it's anything else to do. There aren't any boys and girls clubs or after school programs. Smoking weed is the only way a lot of kids can have safe fun. Weed doesn't make you wanna go do gangsta shit or anything. Just makes you relax. Aint nothing wrong with that.

Before I was smoking weed I can't count the number of dumb shit I was doing to have a good time. I've never been too much of a girly girl. Long as I can remember I've always hung with the guys. Who wants to hang with girls, double dutching and playing with dolls when I could hang with the fellas, chasing the thrill of danger?

Probably one of the most craziest things I can remember doing was opening gates with dogs behind them and letting them chase us. It was all good till one of my old homies, June got caught and a pit bull gnawed on his foot so much that he had to get three toes amputated. So yeah, I think it's safe to say smoking weed was the lesser of evils, considering all I ever wanted to do is eat snacks and crack jokes.

We walked into a spotless crib, thanks to Rod. He told me his Dad had raised him to be some sort of neat freak. Thank God, because me and my Mom both hated cleaning. From the looks of us you'd probably think our crib would be laid out. Paintings on the walls, Fine china, Egyptian rugs, all that fancy shit but naw just your standard furniture, couch, love seat, flat screen , nothing special. We weren't dirty or trifling or anything like that. We made sure the kitchen and bathroom were always up to par. But when it comes to stuff like clothes on the floor or things out a place, we didn't really give a damn. Rod was perfect for us, he kept everything intact.

My Mom was asleep on the couch. I was surprised she was home. Her car was broke down at her man's house a few miles away. Usually that's where she's at. Ever since Rod had moved in a couple weeks back she's been spending more and more time there. I liked it that way. Felt like I had my own crib for once.

Plus I don't feel like she's unsafe when she's there. Like me, my Mom likes to live on the wild side. In all my days on God's Green earth I can never remember her having a real job. Rhonda Parker was a hustler. Never witnessed her personally sell drugs or anything, but nevertheless she was still a hustler.

Her main source of income were Selling Parties. Due to the fact that she was hands down the best cook in Norview, people were always craving her hot plates.

Once she started selling those, she thought why not start selling shots of liquor along with it. The rest was history, our house would be flooded damn near every day. Old heads to youngins, everybody knew about Rhonda's cooking. That lasted for years, until the housing authorities shut it down. They made some rule that anyone having selling parties would be thrown out of their unit.

So we moved everything over to my Aunt Sheila's, her landlord didn't mind. Only problem was, Mom now had to share the profit with her.

Around that time, my Mom begin fucking with nothing but street niggas. Some would move in, some would just come and go, but all, paid these damn bills. What I learned from that was, if a man pays the bills he kinda feels like you're his property. And anytime a man's property doesn't do exactly what they want, they fix it. Fixing usually came with black eyes, or swollen lips. Maybe that's another reason I thought it was ok when I was dealing with Chop. Not sure, but seeing your Mom in pain isn't easy for anyone.

So when my Mom started dating Beenie, I couldn't help but to be overjoyed. He had a nice job, landscaped on the side and even had his own whip. Dude was even a pretty funny guy, I loved him. Beenie doesn't have the heart to hit my Mom. He worshipped the ground she walked on. I was beyond happy for her.

We crept in making sure not to disturb, made our way to my room, sent out a mass text alerting the streets of the new product and awaited our destiny. In no time our phones were ringing off the hook.

We sold everything, dimes dubs, eighths, quarters, half ounces, ounces. Whatever you need, big, medium or small, we had it. Some dealers only sell larger quantities of weed when they cop. I can understand, its less work. Doing it the way we do it requires you to be constantly on the go. But who cares My mama definitely aint raise no lazy bitch. Plus I had Rod with me at all times. It was a great bonding tool.

Only selling large quantities could result in you waiting around all day due to the fact that people don't just wanna spend $300 or better on weed. The faster we sold all the weed, the faster we could go and get more, learned that from Chop. Gotta be honest though, the thought of only selling large quantities did entice me. Think about it, we just paid $2800 for a pound of good smoke, it's usually the more smoke you cop the cheaper the prices were. 2800, was great, beyond great actually. So let's just say someone wanted a quarter of what we had. We can sell it for anywhere from $1000-$1200. Most guys in the city sold them for 1100. But since we got it for so cheap we could sell it for $1000.

Little math lesson; there are 4 quarters in a pound. If we sell four for $1000 a piece than that's $4000. $4000 subtract $2800 is $1200 profit off of four sells. Now remember I said the more weed you bought the cheaper it went for. So if we sold smaller quantity's than our profit would be possibly be up to $2000 more. So for right now we'd continue to sell whatever you need but soon we could upgrade. But only when we have consistent clients who desire large quantities.

See, most so called hustlers around here can't even get to the level of even copping $2800 worth of weed, which is a good thing because that means we had enough to sell them whatever they needed, making us their plug.

 Selling drugs isn't as easy as it seems. It takes great money management skills. Two things most young niggas or bitches don't have. Luckily I do. I made sure we didn't spend shit until we made enough to buy more and as soon as that happened we were calling the plug. Usually we'd still have plenty smoke left, that's called stockpiling. You can never go broke when you have plenty product. Another lesson I learned from Chop.

Within a couple hours of running around town nonstop, we'd made a killing. Even better than we'd expected .With our prices now lower than everyone else's and the fact that we had the best, niggas could score from us and still make a decent come up. Good weed sells itself but this was the quickest we'd ever sold out. I was proud. We called Don and told him to bring us another shipment. He said he'd be a few hours, so we decided to hit up Bahama Breeze, one of my favorite restaurants. We'd made about $1600 in profit. We certainly could afford a little $60 bill.

We pulled up bumpin, 'Gucci Mane". Judging from all of the cars it was a packed house.

"I pray they don't have us waitin all day," I said rubbing my belly.

"You know we could always go to Wendy's, all I'm going to get in here is a burger anyway," said Rod as he turned the ignition off.

"That's your problem, you never wanna step out your realm," I followed, annoyed.

"No, it's not that. I just don't really like trying new things. Why would I order something I've never had, end up not liking it and wasting damn near $30."

"For the experience, fool. For you to be the one from the suburbs you sure don't act like it."

"That's definitely not true. People with money spend it wisely, ghetto people spend it trying to be what they think rich people are," he preached.

"Hold on. Are you tryna call me ghetto," I asked, mistakenly appearing ghetto.

"I mean, if the weave fits," he replied laughing, running his fingers through my Brazilian body wave hair.

"Nigga don't touch my hair. This weave cost more than your life." I joked as we began walking towards the establishment.

I forgot to mention, Rod and I were high as kites. Boy, was that weed the truth. And it's crazy, for some reason whenever I smoked and went inside of a building, everything suddenly started to appear blurry. Even the greeters face.

"Party for two?" asked the blurry faced man.

"Yeah," replied Rod, I looked over and even he was looking funny.

"Right this way," he said as he guided us through the crowded restaurant.

I grabbed Rod's hand. I didn't want to mistakenly bump into anyone and knock their food onto their laps or anything. It was bad enough everything was blurry but the fact that the restaurants lighting was dim definitely didn't do anything to help. Hopefully Rod wasn't feeling how I felt. "Is it me or is the room shaking," I whispered over to him.

"It's you," followed Rod.

"Good," I said under my breath.

"To me it's spinning," he said looking over to me, eyes blood shot.

"Oh my God," I said. Luckily we were seated in a booth quickly without any mishaps.

We casually looked over the menu. Usually I got the Creole Pasta, which was delicious. But tonight I think I wanna try the Jerk Pasta. Caribbean dishes were always my favorite and I'd yet to try this one.

We sat in silence, trapped in our 'high' as the waitress walked up instantly blowing me.

"Can I get you guys anything to drink," she asked, smiling. She was one of those fake ass bitches, fake hair, nails, lashes, brows. Yuck. Don't get me wrong, I've worn all of that too but I only do it on extra special occasions. And trust, I don't have to, I do it because I want. Besides, I could tell this bitch was actually ugly. No amount of makeup could hide those hideous acne scars scattered across her face. I was tempted to pour a gallon of water on her ass to expose her.

Only thing that was authentic on this bitch were her teeth, they were straight, but the hoe probably had to get braces back in the day, she aint fooling me, probably fooling Rod though, guess that's why the troll couldn't help but keep smiling at him. Not once looking over to me.

"Yeah, I'll take a strawberry lemonade," I said firmly, forcing her to take her eyes off my man.

"Yeah. I'll take one too," continued Rod as she quickly smiled back over to him.

"Ok great. I'll be right back. I'll give you guys a second to look over the menu." she said as I rolled my eyes making sure she noticed. I then gave Rod, 'the look'. He most definitely knew what that meant.

"What's wrong bae?" asked Rod.

"You know what the hell is wrong with me nigga," I spat, angrily.

"Actually, I have no idea at all," replied Rod, appearing oblivious.

"Why was that bitch all in your face? Smilin, like I aint sittin right here. And you just lettin her. Keep playin with me and you gonna get your lil girlfriends ass beat," I said sternly, pointing my fork towards him.

"Smiling. At who? Me? When was this?"

"Trevor Alexander Smith, don't play dumb," I warned.

Trevor, was Rod's real name. We only called him Rod because it was short for Dennis 'Rodman'. Everybody in the neighborhood started calling him that because of his colorful hair.

"I swear I don't have a clue what you're talking about," he whined.

"Yeah nigga, whatever. If some dude was just smilin all in my face than you would have a fit."

"What?"

"On second thought maybe you wouldn't," I said, rolling my eyes.

"Hold on what's that supposed to mean. You trying to say I'm soft again?"

"I don't know. If the red hair fits."

"Man I'm.." rod quickly shut up as the waitress came back drinks in hand.

"Here's yours," she said handing one drink over to Rod. "And here's yours," she said placing mine on the table."

I struggled to contain myself. She'd put my drink down so damn hard a tad bit splashed onto my napkin. I took a deep breath. I didn't want shit to get ugly.

"You guys ready to order?" she asked looking over to Rod once more.

"Yes," I strongly stated. "I'll take the Jerk pasta. And give him the Bacon Burger with fries, well done."

Rod, screwed up his face and mouthed the words 'Are you serious' as this dumb bitch had the nerve to look over to him as if she had to check in to see if it was cool. Bitch.

"That's all," I blurted, bringing her attention back over to me.

"Ok. Any appetizers?"

Again this bitch looked over to Rod. Now she was picking with me, causing my blood pressure to sky rocket.

"No, I said that's all," I said, giving her a clue to get the fuck out of here.

"No problem I'll be right back," she said attempting to grab Rods menu. Too bad I snatched it away from her and handed her both of ours at the same time.

She gave a fake smirk before walking away.

"Yo, what the fuck is up with you? You're tripping," said Rod struggling to keep his composure.

"No nigga. You trippin if you think I 'ma let that bitch disrespect me right in front of my face," I said, failing to utilize my inside voice.

"Disrespect?" whispered Rod forcefully.

"Yeah nigga, disrespect," I followed, matching his tone.

"Naw the only thing disrespectful is the way you're treating me."

"What? The way I'm treatin you? You know what you sound like."

"Yeah. A pissed off man," he said before abruptly leaving the table.

"Where the hell you goin?"

"Too the bathroom. If that's ok," He replied sarcastically.

I don't give two fucks what Rod was talking about. That bitch was disrespectful. His ass should've straightened her out and I would've never had to take control. He always on that soft punk ass shit. You'd think he was the one with the pussy. I was growing more aggravated by the moment. On top of that my high was completely gone. I needed a drink. As always I snuck in a half pint bottle of Cîroc in my purse. I'll be damned if I pay them high ass drink prices when I can bring my own. My family had been doing this for years. Of course Rod hated when I did it but that aint never stop him from taking any.

I sucked down some of my drink, leaving room to pour the Cîroc, looked around before placing the bottle and glass under the table and poured. Closing off the bottle, I used my straw to mix it around before sucking the entire drink down. Damn I needed that.

By the time Rod came back I had a slight buzz due to the fact I'd lost control of myself and poured Cîroc in his drink before gulping it down. I'd also demanded a different waiter. I was now ready to enjoy our date. Fuck that bitch.

"You mad at me baby?" I asked.

"You drunk my drink?" he asked, annoyed, holding his empty glass in the air.

"Yeah but I got our new waiter to bring some more, relax," I said batting my eyes. As usual the liquor was bringing out my alter ego. Angelica. I always got super horny whenever I'm intoxicated and right now Rod was looking like a cock strong bull that I wanted to ride.

"Ok," Rod said, attempting to keep it brief. Luckily I knew exactly what to do to break the ice. I slipped off my right Ugg boot with my left foot and slid my feet across the table onto his crotch.

"Whoa. What are you doing?" he whispered.

I sat silent continuing to bat my eyes as I bit the right corner of my bottom lip, massaging his dick with my toes slowly.

"Chill out," he said unsuccessfully attempting to remove my foot.

I mouthed the word 'nope' as I continued massaging, staring him dead in the eyes.

"I'm serious. This aint the time."

"You gonna be nice to me?" I asked as I felt his penis enlarging.

"Yeah. Everything's cool," he said looking around. "People can see you."

"So," I replied, continuing to look him in the eyes. "You gonna fuck me when we get home?" I asked provocatively.

"Yes Candy," said Rod softly, continuing to look around.

"You gonna fuck me good?" I asked as I undressed him with my eyes.

"Yes baby."

"You promise?" I asked, blowing him a kiss.

"Yes I promise. Just chill right now. It's not the place," said Rod as he grew visibly nervous.

"So you telling me you don't want me to sneak under the table and suck that big ol dick?"

"No," he said, shocked. "Are you crazy?"

"No? Are you sure? Cause someone seems to think differently," I replied as his dick grew even larger.

"Baby chill."

"Nope," I replied as I slowly began sliding my body under the table.

"We got your order up and ready," our new waiter, a chubby white man said as he carried our food in his hands while another chubby black guy followed with the refills.

I then mouthed the words "You're lucky' as I erotically licked my lips, removing my foot from his privates, leaving him with a look of relief.

For the next thirty minutes Rod and I ate our food, which was de-fucking-licious I might add and finished off the remainder of the Cîroc. By the time we were done we were wasted and full. What a great combination. Oh yeah can't forget to mention we were both undeniably horny. The liquor was getting the best of us and Angelica was growing unruly.

"Where the fuck is the waiter? I'm ready to jump on that dick," I asked as I searched around.

"And I'm ready for you to jump on it. Where the fuck is he?" asked Rod, looking around also. "Seems like we've been waiting here for centuries."

"You wanna walk out?" I asked.

"Without paying?" Rod blurted.

"Shhh," I said looking around. "Yeah. You've never done it before?" I whispered.

"Hell no."

"You scared?"

"No," Rod said hesitantly. Yep there was no doubt he was drunk. The sober Rod would never agree to this.

"Let's go."

"Right now?" he asked, observing our surroundings.

"Yeah nigga," I followed as I looked around also. "Aint nobody even paying us any attention. The coast is clear."

"Let's do it," Rod said as he took in a deep breath.

I grabbed my purse and made my way to the door, leaving Rod to follow. We walked smoothly passed all customers and employees as no one seemed to notice. In no time we were home free, walking out the door. The next step was the car. I picked up the pace, never once looking back. When out of nowhere we heard a voice from a distance.

"Yo," screamed a man from behind us.

"Oh shit Candy," they caught us. "Are we going to jail? You're already out on bail. Damn man. We just should've just paid. Fuck," stuttered Rod.

"Chill, just keep walkin," I followed.

"Keep walking? Let's just pay them," said Rod as he frantically searched inside his pants pocket."

Too late, the footsteps of feet jogging over to us began to get closer. Usually I would have a plan on what to do right now. But not today. Candy was the smart one, not Angelica.

"Ay bro," said a stranger from inches away.

We both turned around ready to face the consequences. To our surprise it was the guy from the booth behind us. "Bro you left your wallet," he said, smiling.

"Oh shit," Rod and I said simultaneously, relieved.

"Thanks man," Rod said as he grabbed the wallet. "Appreciate it."

"No problem man. I know you would've been mad about losing that," he said before making his way back into the restaurant.

"Damn that was close," said Rod as he flopped down onto the trunk of our car.

We headed home. Hopefully my Mom would be gone by now. Angelica was in full swing and I was ready to get loud and nasty.

Just our luck, we get home and she's still there. Only this time she had suitcases in the middle of the living room, packing.

"Mom what are you doin?" I asked as I surveyed the house. "What's goin on? Where you goin?"

"I'm getting the hell out here. That's where the hell I'm goin," she replied. She had on pajama pants, her leather jacket and a bonnet over her head. This had to be serious. My Mom never left the house without looking up to par. She was only 37, slim and appeared no older than 30. She prided herself on looking better than these young girls walking around here. She'd never step out like this. Whatever's going on had to be serious.

"What happened Ma?" I asked visibly concerned.

"Somebody tried to rob yall that's what the fuck happened," My mom snapped.

"What?" I shouted.

"Are you serious? How?" Followed Rod.

"Yes, I'm serious. I'm on the couch asleep and some nigga busted up in here. Guess they picked the lock and I was too far gone in my sleep to hear anything," she said looking around as if to make sure she had everything she needed. "When I screamed, they ran. They ass probably thought no one was home because my car parked at Beenie's"

"Did you see who it was?" I asked, holding back tears. It kills me to see my Mom in any kind of distress.

"Hell no I didn't. I told you I was half sleep. I know they was black. That's about it. They nearly scared me half to death. But fuck this yall can have this house I'm going to stay with my man. Fuck this. I aint got time," she said, talking with her hands as a horn blew. "That's probably him right there."

"Ma. So you just gonna leave me?" I asked as she peeked out of the window.

Yeah, I know she stays at Beenie's a lot but I've never officially lived away from her. Sure, the rent was income based so I could afford it but I'm just not ready to officially live without my Mommy.

"Yep," she said before picking up two suitcases.

"You need any help?" asked Rod walking over, attempting to assist her.

"Nope I got it," she added as she walked over to the door. "I took everything that was valuable to me," she said, looking back at us. "I'll come get the rest later. Yall two better be safe. Everybody aint your damn friend. Remember that," she said as she walked out of the house. "Bye," she said slamming the door.

"What the fuck? Who could have done this?" I questioned as I paced the room. "It better not have been Nhi and his fake ass friends."

"I doubt it was him. Could've been anyone," followed Rod as he looked around. "You thinking about slowing down with the weed?"

"Hell naw. I'm thinking about popping a nigga," I replied furiously.

"Baby chill."

"Naw fuck that. Aint no chillin. Niggas think cause I'm a girl I'm soft. Naw aint no hoe in my blood." I said fuming, still pacing. "And your ass gettin a gun too. You think niggas won't run up on you," I barked.

"Baby. A gun isn't the answer. We just have be safe. Keep all our business to our self and get better locks on the door," he said calmly, pointing to the standard lock on the door. "All we have to do is play smarter. Don't trip. The good thing is that they didn't get anything and no one was hurt."

I stood shaking my head. I'm not sure if I was actually that mad or the liquor was causing me to be extra emotional as I felt a tear drop down my cheeks.

"Baby everything's going to be ok," said Rod easing his way closer to me. He stood in front of me, pulling me close, wrapping his loving arms around my body as he kissed me upon my forehead. "We in this together baby aint nothing else gonna happen. I promise," he said as he began delicately kissing and sucking my neck, rubbing his gentle hands carefully up and down my backside, causing my pussy to suddenly grow a heartbeat. My panties began sticking as my love oozed from inside of me. Unbuckling my bra strap, he continued to lick and suck my neck before lifting my shirt from me as my bra fell to my feet.

It was then that he eased me over to the couch, never once taking his hands away from my body, laying me down, feasting on my pencil sharp nipples as he carefully removed my jeans and panties. With every second that passed my body yearned for him to simply rub his dick over my clit.

Once I was completely naked, he passionately made love to me with his eyes as he removed his shirt, revealing his flawless physique before returning, licking my entire body slowly, caressing me with his pillow soft hands. I lightly moaned as I feigned for him to touch the one spot he'd ignored. Still, he took his time. The anticipation was killing me as my body shook and trembled. Realizing I could no longer take the pressure we locked eyes before he dived face first into my ocean, taking his precious time navigating his way to the promise land. As he discovered my hidden treasure I screamed in pleasure as my body erupted.

Rod then stood triumphantly, over top of me, still fully dressed minus his shirt. "Get in that room," he demanded. Wasting no time I followed his orders, diving onto the bed. He slowly followed without muttering a sound as I sat patiently on the edge of the bed, legs cocked, silent studying every inch of his body as he slowly undressed. I closed my eyes, rubbing my throbbing juice box clockwise.

Upon opening my eyes, Rod stood naked, directly in front of me. Dick at full attention, gripping a wad of cash in his possession before abruptly tossing the money into the air, ones, tens, fives, twenty's, fifty's and hundreds leisurely made their way on and around the bed. Never in my life had I been so worked up. If someone would have told me Jesus was standing in front of me I would never have questioned them. Fuck anything and everything, this moment was all that mattered.

I slid further back onto the bed as Rod crawled unhurriedly towards me like the king of the Jungle seeking his prey.

Fuck who ever tried to break into the house. They couldn't stop what we got going on. Me and my baby got this. You can bet that.

ATLANTA

Operation: Get to Atlanta was a success! We'd had the Midas touch. Everything hadn't just gone as planned, it had gone even better. The weed game in Norview was ours! In less than a week, most, if not all competition had become faithful customers. We were reliable and cheaper. How could you beat that? Don had quickly become our best friend.

Still never found out who'd broken in the spot but we added a security system and extra locks to the door, so we were straight. Life was great. This trip wasn't only needed, it was well deserved.

We'd just checked into our hotel, The Ritz Carlton. I would tell you it was top notch but that would be an understatement. It was immaculate, too dope, the room, excuse me maybe I should call it by its proper name, The Palace, was remarkable, Clear view of the entire city, King Size Bed with the softest plush 400 count cotton linen, and a 37 inch smart T.V. plastered on the wall. The bathroom came equip with marble floors and a walk in shower with the rain shower head. While the living room which was separated by two double doors had a pull out couch, full mini bar and an even bigger TV. This was a far stretch from the Ramada Inn I was used to staying in.

And I haven't even mentioned the best part. Guess how much we paid for it? Come on, just guess! You'll never believe it. $200 for two fucking nights! A five star telly for $200 a night. Unbelievable. Rod had really come through this time. Him and his family vacationed a lot growing up and he knew about some website where you can name your price for a hotel, choose the state, quality and Voila! They'd find you s spot. Crazy Right?

So yeah, we'd through all of our bags in the room and were now off to the world famous Lenox Mall. We'd heard rappers shouting it out for years and couldn't wait to tear it down. My purse held ten thousand dollars cash and we were prepared to go home with nothing. Why not? It was guaranteed we'd make it back in no time.

I stepped into the mall instantly mesmerized. I thought Military Circle mall back home got crazy on Fridays but it was obvious I didn't know a damn thing. This place was ridiculously packed from wall to wall. If it's one thing I'd noticed while I was here it was the fact that everyone around appeared to be balling. While Rod and I still sported the comfy sweats and sneakers we'd traveled in everyone else dressed similar to a black high school on the first day back after Christmas break. Never in my life had I seen anything like it. Where did they get the money to shop like this? But never mind all that, this place was a shop-a-holics dream. My eyes lit up. I'd died and went to Heaven.

No wonder them Instagram famous bitches from Atlanta always on point. How could you not? Pure, Ugg store, Fendi, Neiman Marcus, Mcm, all stores that I had never even knew existed. I stared in astonishment as Rod and I bumped and slid our way through the overly crowded mall.

"Oooh I wanna go in there," I said, excitedly pointing to the 'Steve Madden' store. "No, never mind, let's go there first," I said after switching my attention over to the 'Louis Vuitton' store.

Rod didn't seem nearly as enthused as I did. I figured he'd be like this though. He liked clothes and he was a nice dresser but he was more into ordering gear offline and things of that nature. "Ok. Baby just slow down, you're walking so fast, I'm going to lose you."

"Well nigga you better keep up, shit," I said as I speeded towards the store.

"Are you even going to buy anything in there?" he asked, from behind me.

"I don't know. I might. Why?" I asked as I continued walking, never looking back.

"Don't forget we're not rich."

"Boy shut up," I said as I shot into the store. Not rich? Yeah I may not be rich but let's not forget I have ten racks in my purse. That nigga tripping, always being a damn party pooper, should've left his ass in the hotel.

His opinion was irrelevant due to the fact that seconds later I'd completely forgotten he was even behind me. To be honest I'd forgotten anyone was. I'd suddenly blossomed into a bonafide super star, it was as though an ultra-bright spotlight had been shined upon me as I glided through the entrance of the store. My freshly done faux lox flowed gracefully as if the perfect gush of wind had hit me. All attention focusing on me.

I was fully prepared to walk out empty handed, head in the sky. No, not because I wasn't buying anything but because I was ready to buy so much that the workers were going to have to escort me to my car as they held my many luxurious bags in their possession.

Gorgeous purses, shoes, dresses, accessories, kill me now! I'd seen it all, I thought as I made my way over to the most beautiful Gloss Red Leather purse I'd ever witnessed with my own two eyes. I stood inches away, admiring its undeniable beauty, this was the purse of a boss, a purse made just for me, a purse that would surely let everyone back home know that we were different and they could never, ever get on my level, a purse that was $5000! "Oh hell naw," I

shouted as I snapped back into reality.

"What babe? What's wrong?" Rod asked, startling me.

"Nothing. Let's get out here. I don't see anything I want," I exclaimed as I

shot to the nearest exit.

Fuck that, I hate to admit but Rod was right, we aint rich. I guess the thought

of purchasing whatever I wanted was cool but that thought is long gone. I'm not

sure how much weed we were going to have to sell to afford shit like that but I

know we weren't even close to reaching that point yet.

We stepped back into the jungle. Only this go around it was time to act my

wage, which wasn't too bad considering the fact that their Forever 21 was huge

and they stocked a ton more than the one back home. This was great because I'd

still be able to flex on all the Norview hoes. Not to mention they had a huge sale.

Can you say winning!

"You ok baby?" I asked Rod as we walked out of 'Wet Seal' probably our

hundredth store. Both our hands were filled with bags from the various stores we'd

conquered. I could tell he was becoming annoyed.

"Yeah I guess. You ready yet?" he asked as he held on tightly to my bags, struggling to stand clear of the hundreds of shoppers stampeding around us.

"Ready? We didn't even get anything you wanted yet."

"Baby its cool. I'm just ready to get the fuck out of here," he whined as we walked side by side.

"You sure?" I asked.

"Yeah I have clothes at the hotel. Plus I don't think we have any more room for me to get anything else," he said as he raised the bags up.

"Ok," I followed as we steered our way through the mall's exit.

Walking to our vehicle was like strolling through a car show. Never before had I seen so many luxury vehicles at one time. Bentleys, hummers, and lambs all sat parked, sparkling as the glow from the sun pleasured my eyes. It's safe to say I was in awe. I looked over to Rod. He clearly didn't share the same sentiments. Instead he appeared exhausted, like a guy who'd worked hard labor for fifteen hours and was forced to walk 30 miles home in the pouring rain. But who cares? Not me. He's my nigga, which means he's supposed to cater to me.

We finally arrived to the car.

"Yo," hollered a guy parked a couple cars to the left of us. He stepped out his BMW appearing to be probably a few years older than us.

"Yo," replied Rod suspiciously as he opened his driver side back door, tossing our bags inside.

"Yall know I got everything you need right hea," he said with a deep southern drawl as he walked over to the trunk, he'd just popped.

"Naw we good," I followed as I opened the front passenger seat door. Aint no way in hell I would allow us to get robbed in Atlanta. Who knows what he has in his trunk. I'm far from stupid and pretty sure he didn't own anything of interest to me. My Mama always told me to beware of wolves in sheep's clothing and although he was rocking Robin jeans, shirt, paints, hat, and jacket with crisp Jordan 11's to match, I'm still almost positive all that simply was a disguise. Nine times out a ten he's a robber, looking to finesse his way into our pockets. Sucks for him, I'm from the hood, can't fool me. Hell, he probably got all that gear from robbing some other innocent couple.

"I'm serious shawty. All that shit they got in the mall, I got right hea for the low low," he added as he continued pointing into his trunk. "Naw foreal. Ask about me. Erbody know me I'm Westside P," he replied confidently.

"It's ok, we're good," Followed Rod as he opened his driver's side door.

"You tellin me you don't want none of these new Robin jeans?" he asked as he held a black pair to the sky. "They official tissue, no bullshit Shawty, I know yall see me rockin em. I look like a nigga who rock fugazi shit? Hell naw," he replied answering his own question. "You makin a big mistake, I'm tryna tell you," he said still raising the jeans up as Rod and I both stood in the doorways to the car, listening. "You don't wanna just check em out? It can't hurt."

Gotta admit, the nigga did have a point. Robin jeans go from about four hundred beans to as much as a thousand dollars. As a matter of fact, you can't even find them in VA, you gotta order them online. Atlanta was one of few that actually had them on deck.

"How much are they?" asked Rod.

"Shit, nothin but a ball fifty. You can't beat it. What size you wear? You look like bout a 34," he said as he searched through his merchandise.

"Yeah. That's right," followed Rod.

"See, I told you I do this shit. I got three different colors in 34. Official shit. Come look," he said motioning for us to come over. Rod and I looked at one another. "Man yall don't gotta be all nervous. I see the Virginia tags. I know yall probably thinkin I'm on some crazy shit but trust me, all I'm tryna do is give yall the deal of a life time. Real spill."

I nodded to Rod. Guess it would be ok to check out his inventory. Still, I made sure my right hand clutched the pistol in my purse. Won't catch me slipping today.

Once we got closer I got a better look at him. His lips were dark, probably from smoking and he had bags under his eyes. He actually appeared a little older than I initially thought but who knows he might just be one of those young guys who lived a rough life.

"What one you like my boy?" he asked holding the three jeans in front of us as Rod carefully examined them. "So, what yall just down hea on a little vacation or somethin?"

"Yeah," said Rod.

"No doubt. No doubt. You see any you like?"

"I like these ones," followed Rod, pointing to the pair that I didn't particularly care for. For some reason I knew he'd pick those. Not saying they were ugly. I just knew he wasn't gonna go with the ones I'd been eyeing. They were light blue with what looked like bleach stains splattered all over with gold pockets on the back, simply gorgeous. Instead, he chose the plain ol regular ass black ones with black pockets and silver rhinestones on the back. I mean, they were cool, I guess.

"Bet. You sure you don't want another pair?" asked Westside.

"Naw this is enough," replied Rod.

"You sure? I can give you the two for two hundred special," he asked. "Come on shawty you know you can't beat that price. Best in the world."

"Yeah but..," Rod said hesitantly. I prayed he'd said yes. And before you go thinking we're stupid. Trust, we know the jeans are fake. Well, at least I do. I'm not dumb enough to believe someone would be selling exclusive jeans like those, more than half off. It's just that everyone back home knew we were coming to Atlanta and had been getting money lately. Aint no way they weren't gonna think they were official. Plus I'd been looking over them and they're perfect. Trust me I know how fake jeans usually look.

The ones in the 'Bills Flea Market' back home are the worse. Stitching all fucked up, designer symbols in the wrong place, shit, I've even seen a pair of jeans that had Tru Religion spelled True Realigion. I swear. So yeah like I said these were just fine. Besides, I've always been taught 'Sometimes you just gotta fake it until you make it'.

"Come on my boy, you know this the deal of a lifetime. Hell, you can even take them back to Va. and sell them for double. You look like a hustla, I know you can flip it." said Westside.

Rod looked over to me. I nodded. This nigga Westside was a damn good persuader. I'm impressed.

"It's only $50 more," I added.

"Yeah you're right," said Rod. "I'll take those pair," he said, pointing.

Damn! I couldn't believe he still chose the pair I didn't want him to have. This time the jeans were just plain ol dark blue with gold pockets on the back with gold rhinestones. A part of me wanted to just cop the jeans that I liked myself but I decided not to. His ass probably wouldn't wear them anyway.

"Fo sho," Westside said as Rod handed him over the cash. I made sure my hand gripped my pistol tightly just in case he tried to pull a fast one.

Everything was cool though. "Oh yeah, yall know I got that official molly," he added as he passed Rod the jeans.

"How much," I asked.

"$25 for a half gram. And shit is a missile. Got the whole city going crazy. I got two bags left. How yall gon act? I know yall wanna pipe up in the city. Aint nobody never had no fun being sober."

"Yeah you're right, we'll take both of them," said Rod after looking over to me, seeing that I was interested.

"Boy yall the shit. I swear yall about to be high as a kite," he said surveying our surroundings as he reached into his pocket, delivering a smooth hand to hand transaction over to Rod.

"So what yall plan on doing tonight?"

"Honestly we have no idea. All we know is that we definitely tryna hit a strip club before we leave," I said.

"Oh than you're talkin to the right man," said Westside as he pounded his fist to his chest. "I know where shit pop every night. Let me see," he said appearing to be thinking. "What's today?"

"Friday," replied Rod.

"Friday, oh shit, well Tropical gonna be lit tonight. Erbody gonna be in that bitch. Real shit. And them hoes," he screamed excitedly. "Them hoes is off the mothafuckin chain in that bitch. I don damn near had all of them," he said before remembering that I was a girl. "Excuse me Ms. Lady I aint tryna disrespect you." I guess southern hospitality was real. Back home a nigga didn't care what he said in front of a female. Not that I cared, just different.

"Oh trust me I don't mind. I been around hoes all my life," I followed. "So you tellin me that's definitely where we need to be tonight?"

"Most definitely. Matter fact you probably see my black ass in there. That's sort of my way of giving back to the community."

"Huh," I asked as Rod and I both laughed.

"Yeah, see, I think of it like this. I'm throwin money at these hoes," he looked at me, "Excuse me, I'm throwin money at these women and they taking that money, payin bills, buyin pampers. Shit, even if they going to get a bag of coke or molly, I'm still helpin the nigga they scorin from. I look at it as if it's comin full circle. All I'm doing is my part in helpin the economy stay poppin."

Rod and I continued laughing. "I guess I can understand that," followed Rod.

"Fo sho, fo sho. I hope I see yall there. If I don't I just want you to know it was nice meetin yall and welcome to the city. Enjoy. Just be safe. Don't let the glitz and glamour of Atlanta confuse you. It's some real cut throat niggas out hea ready to pray on out towners," he preached. "You aint gotta worry about me though. I'm sort of like Ezel, except it's not that I steal, its I hustle, I don't kill," he rapped before making his way to his driver's side door. "Peace out."

"Alright bro. Appreciate it," said Rod.

"See ya," I followed before we made our wake back over to our whip, forgetting I'd failed to ask him an essential question. "Ay. You know where the house Gucci Mane grew up in is at?" I asked, turning back around.

"You talkin bout over there in East Atlanta?" he asked, looking back to us as he opened his driver's side door.

"Yeah," I replied as I grew excited.

"Hell yeah I know. 1017 Longhorn Street. His apartments closed down though. All boarded up and shit. Yall can still ride by though," replied Westside.

"I don't even care. I just want to see it," I quickly replied.

"Yeah I understand. Gucci's the king. Some people come to Atlanta just to see it. But just be careful when you go. Don't forget I told you them jack boys be lurkin."

"Trust me we gonna be good," I said.

"Bet. It's about thirty minutes away. Yall got GPS don't you?"

"Yep."

"Cool. Well like I said. Be safe and I might see yall later," he said, hopping in his whip, closing the door.

We finally sat down as Rod cranked up the tunes before skating off.

"So baby. You wanna go to Tropical tonight?" I asked turning down the music.

"Yeah that's cool," said Rod unenthused.

"Damn. You not excited?"

"Yeah. I guess I am," replied Rod showing no change of demeanor.

"You get on my fuckin nerves," I snapped.

"What did I do? What are you talking about?"

"Nigga, turn up sometime. Act excited for a change. You make me feel like we came here for nothin. Always so nonchalant, 'Yeah I guess'," I said in my mocking voice.

"Wooo," Rod screamed. "Is that excited enough? What do you want me to do?"

"Fucking Bitch," I mumbled staring straight ahead.

"Yo. Candy, for the last time. Stop calling me out of my name."

"Stop doin shit that requires me to call you out your name."

"You want everything your way. And the crazy thing is. I try to give you whatever you want and you still complain. Maybe it just isn't any pleasing you," Rod vented.

"Whatever."

Seriously. This nigga always working my nerves. Part of the reason I fuck with the guy is because the fact less is more with him. He says less, dresses less and does less to impress people. But still, there are those times when I'm just like Nigga, living up a little. Guess I'm just used to being surrounded by hood and ghetto people. Maybe I'm the one who should change.

Who am I kidding, I aint changing shit. His ass better work on it. Or at least try to improve. I'm getting sick and tired of being all hype by my damn self. Ol voice of reason ass nigga, cool calm collected ass nigga. His lollipop head ass act like he perfect or something. Nigga need to learn to appreciate what the fuck he got. His ass lucky he got a real deal hustler instead of one of them broke gossiping ass hoes who be running around Norview. I'm one in a million and he better start acting like it. Hmmph.

"Take me to McDonalds." I demanded. All that shopping had worked up my appetite.

"Ok," Rod said as we approached one a little further ahead.

"I wanted to go to a real restaurant. But I know you probably don't want too. We might spend too much money or somethin," I said still never looking over to him.

He didn't reply, simply shook his head. I'd noticed from looking over to him from the corner of my eye. Should go out without his ass tonight. His cheap self probably one of them niggas who throw a couple dollars then, sneaks it back by dragging it with his foot when no one's looking.

As we pulled into McDonalds the drive thru was wrapped around the building, we decided to walk in only to find out that it was packed on the inside too. I'm starting to think everywhere we'd go in this city would be like this.

With all these customers they still had the nerve to only have one register open. We stood in the back of the line, I stepped ahead of him. I didn't feel like ordering my food with his ass. I was completely annoyed and I wasn't afraid to show it.

After what seemed like an eternity I finally got the chance to order my food. I got my usual, ten piece nugget and fries. I left Rod to order his alone. Time drug as I leaned onto the counter, nearly dozing off as I impatiently awaited the food.

"Order 572," called out a Filipino worker. I looked down to my receipt and it was me. 'About time' I thought.

"Thanks," I said to the cashier as I retrieved the grub. I should've gotten them to throw in something extra for the wait but I decided not to press the issue.

I made my way to the opposite end of the counter where the straw and napkin dispenser were located. Grabbed what I needed before realizing I'd forgotten my sweet and sour sauce. I made my way back over to where the cashier was. There's no way possible I could eat nuggets without them.

"Excuse me. I asked for sweet and sour sauce and I didn't get any," I said to a middle aged Filipino woman.

"Where is your receipt?" she asked with a foreign accent.

"My receipt? You just handed me my food 30 seconds ago," I replied, attempting to remain calm. There were a lot of people in the restaurant and I didn't want to cause a scene.

"Yes but I do not remember what you ordered. Only nuggets come with sauce. Any other time it is .25 cent each." I rolled my eyes as I handed her the receipt. She read over it slowly as if she was taking a damn test or something. "Ok," she said before reaching under the counter to retrieve two packets of sauce. "Have a nice day," she followed, handing me the sauce and receipt, bearing a fake smile.

I snatched the items and turned around only to realize I'd left my food unattended at the other end of the counter. Too late. I looked around for Rod. "You seen my food?" I asked spotting him walking up to the cashier.

"No," he said as he grabbed his meal from the Filipino lady.

"Where the fuck is my food?" I asked aloud as I slowly surveyed the room.

"I don't know. What do you mean? Where did you put it?" asked Rod as he now stood in front of me.

"I left it right there," I said pointing to the napkins and straws. "All I was tryna do was get some sweet and sour sauce, turned around and it was fuckin gone."

"I don't know babe. You think someone took it?"

"Duh. Where else could it be?" I said as I continued looking around.

"Just tell the cashier what happened. I'm sure she'll understand."

Customers slowly began to glance over to me one by one as my anger had obviously become noticeable.

"Somebody stole my damn food," I barked to the workers behind the counter.

"I'm sorry. Would you like to get back in line," replied the dumb ass Filipino lady as she pointed over to the now even more crowded line.

"Get back in line. Bitch, did you hear me? I said somebody stole my fuckin food," I shouted as I pressed my body against the edge of the counter making sure I was as close as physically possible. "I need some more. Yall know I just bought my shit. Don't play with me. What kinda business yall runnin? Got thieves walkin all up in here," I continued, fuming. "Do yall got any cameras in here I'm about to beat some fuckin ass," I said turning around to the customers. Funny, they all seemed to be checking their phones as if they hadn't been looking at me. "Yall must don't know who the fuck yall dealin with," I barked. I'd become so angry tears were starting to form at the corners of my eyes. It wasn't just the fact that I never and I mean ever play when it comes down to my food but let us not forget Rod had already pissed me off.

"Sorry. We can't do anything about that," followed the Filipino lady once more. Only this time she was smiling.

"What? What the fuck you mean you can't do anything about it. Bitch you better give me some more food."

"Sorry ma'am," she said as she looked away. "Order 577," she added as she held up a customer's food.

"UUUUHHH," I screamed as I began pacing.

"Baby its ok. I'll buy you some more," said Rod attempting to grab my arm.

"Get the Fuck off me," I said throwing his hands off of me. "I don't want anymore. I want what I just had. And these motherfuckers let somebody steal it," I said looking back, pointing at the Filipino lady, who was still smiling.

"Ma'am no one told you to leave your food unattended," replied the Filipino lady.

"What bitch? I'll fuck your ass up. Fuck wrong with you?" I said peering deep into her eyes, as I lost all patience. I suddenly felt a light tap on my shoulder.

"Excuse me. Could you cut out the curse words?" an elderly white man asked as he pointed over to two small children standing beside him.

"Fuck you," I blurted. "I'm a grown ass woman," I replied as the man turned back around giving one of those fake ass white people smirks they do when they don't know what to say next.

I grew enraged as I tossed my sweet and sour sauces at the cashier before storming out as Rod followed. I flew over to the car just to find out it was locked and I had to wait for him.

"Yo you're tripping," he said as he opened the car door. "That shit was embarrassing. What's up with you?"

"Nigga if I embarrass you so much then don't talk to me, it's simple," I replied flopping into the car.

"What? Are you serious? Do you hear the words that you're saying? You need anger management. You got problems," he said, forcefully sticking the key into the ignition.

"Naw nigga your daddy got problems."

"What? Why would you say that?" asked Rod angrily.

Damn why did I just say that? I'm stupid, always taking things too far. That was a low blow. Rods dad did in fact have problems. Serious ones. Actually that's the reason he was even in Virginia in the first place. He'd told me his Dad was a war vet turned drug addict. He suffered from Post-Traumatic Stress Syndrome, resulting in him abusing Rod mentally and physically. Over the years it had gotten so bad he had no choice but to move here with his Aunt while his mom seeked helped for his Dad. He told me his story in confidence and I through it back in his face. "I'm sorry," I said remorseful.

Rod sat silent.

"Did you hear me? I said I'm sorry."

"What the fuck is wrong with you? You do whatever the hell you want to people and then think its ok by just saying sorry. Fuck that. You need to grow the hell up. Everything can't be Candy's way," said Rod. His anger was causing him to drive aggressively.

I sat speechless. Ironically I enjoyed this side of him. Taking authority. Not being a little bitch and letting me run over top of him. He needed to do this more often. I had become completely turned on. "I really am sorry baby. I know I have to do better. I'm going to work on it. I promise." He still sat silent. "You hear me baby? I promise," I said as I rubbed his thigh. "I don't know what gets into me." I wasn't lying. I knew I shouldn't have snapped in there but I always had a problem with my anger and controlling it. Maybe he was right, maybe I should look into some anger management classes or something. Over reacting is usually my first reaction. "You wanna smoke," I asked as I pulled out an already rolled blunt from my purse. "I already rolled it and everything," I said as I held the perfectly rolled spliff to the ceiling.

"Sure. I need it," he replied shaking his head.

"Cool," I said, trying my best to be sexy. I always do that when I know I'm wrong. "So where do you want to go now?"

"Doesn't really matter to me," Rod said nonchalantly.

"Let's go to East Atlanta."

"For what?"

"To see Gucci's old crib. Duh," I said excitedly.

"Oh yeah. I forgot about that. Ok. I don't care."

Rod typed in the address and we made our way over. But first we had to make a pit stop at Burger King. Only this time we went through the drive thru. I didn't want to cause any more problems so I sat quietly as Rod gave the cashier my money. Once we left, we lit the blunt and hit the road.

After about a 30 minute drive we finally drove past a sign that read 'East Atlanta'. Even the slightest Gucci fan knows that's his former stomping grounds. "You smell that baby?" I asked Rod as I rolled down the window.

"Eww. What? Did you fart again?" he asked as he rolled down his window.

"No," I replied. "I'm talking about East Atlanta. It smells exactly how I imagined it would," I said with my nose to the air.

"You know you're crazy don't you," followed Rod, smirking.

"I'm dead ass. This is a dream come true. I've always dreamed of coming here. This is better than Disney World. Thank you for comin with me baby," I said smiling over to him.

"Are you serious? It's actually not at all what I expected. Whatsup with all these big houses and kids riding on skateboards. I thought it would be a little more hood than this."

"Relax. We still haven't gotten to his old crib. Just sit back and enjoy the scenery. Oh shit, look baby." We both looked over to my left as I pointed. "I bet you that's the Texaco he used to hustle in front of back in the day. He raps about that all the time."

"You think so?"

"Shit I don't know. Maybe."

I sat smiling. This was so special to me. Gucci was such an inspiration. For him to be just a regular hood nigga and for his influence to spread across the world was amazing. I know he isn't the only person who's done great things from the ghetto but I'm absolutely in love with his work ethic. Even now that he's in jail he still has countless mixtapes and albums that seem to drop every day. It's obvious he worked his ass off when he was home. How could anyone not look at that as motivation? It's gotta be an amazing feeling to wake up every morning and do what you want. If I could ever find something I was passionate about like he is to rap, I'd be the same way. Most girls probably look up to corny people like Oprah or something. Yeah, guess that's cool but I'm more of the Gucci type. He does it his way or the highway and even if the world doesn't fully appreciate him now. I'd bet my last dollar he's gonna die a legend, ultimately living forever. To me that's priceless.

We pulled into a neighborhood that looked completely different from the homes we'd just seen. This was the ghetto. Grassless lawns, trash scattered and boarded up houses, bando's is what they called them around here. Usually drug dealers sold their drugs out of them. But the hood looked pretty dead right now. Not a soul in site. A few cars were parked but more than half the houses and apartments were bando's. Still, this was the East Atlanta I wanted to see. I pulled out my phone to take pictures. I kinda hoped people would be standing on the corners, shooting dice, drinking, I guess it was a good thing that they weren't but I could've stood a little action.

"Pull over. Pull over," I shouted as the GPS told us 'We'd Arrived' at Gucci's old spot. It was a two story brick apartment building. Still, I had to take a closer look. I hopped out the second Rod pulled up to the curb.

"Baby. What are you doing?" asked Rod.

I ignored him as I thought about all my favorite Gucci songs that were inspired during the time he'd lived here. This was even better than everything I'd bought at the mall. Probably even better than the strip club. I must've taken a hundred selfies in front of his old address '1017'.

"Baby I need you," I said running over to the car.

"Need me for what?" asked Rod from the driver's seat. "I need someone to take pictures for me. I can't only take selfies. Plus, me and you have to take a selfie together next to the address sign. Come on," I whined.

"Do we have to?"

"Yes. Are you crazy. I thought you loved Gucci Mane too."

"I do but I'm just not a fanatic."

"Well sorry. I am. Come on," I said rushing back over to the house.

Rod followed. Of course he was nervous. I didn't care though. I was on cloud 9. We took pictures, smiling, mean mugging and making silly faces before we headed back to the car.

"See, this wasn't so bad. Don't tell me that wasn't fun," I said as I flopped down in the seat.

"Yeah. Tons of fun," Rod said sarcastically as he snapped on his seatbelt. Then, out of the darkness we shockingly received a tap on the wind shield.

"Oh Shit," rod blurted, dropping the car keys between his seat and the armrest as a gold mouthed goon gazed through the window. Eyes bloodshot, skin, blending with the dark sky.

Rod frantically searched for the keys as the goon spoke. "Chill bruh. I aint come to do nothin," said the Southern Goon from outside the window.

Fuck that I thought as I grabbed my gun from my pure. I aint getting Robbed in front of Gucci house. Hell naw, back in the day Gucci smoked a nigga for trying to rob him and I was prepared to do the exact same thing. I don't care.

"We're good bro," followed Rod as I gripped tightly to my pistol. I shouldn't have to tell you he was visibly shaking in his boots. I can't blame him this time. What a time to lose the keys.

"Bruh," he said before pulling out a pocket full of money. "I aint tryna rob yall. I'm straight. I'm Twin from Bankhead. Erbody know me. I'm just out here stalkin my girl."

Why did everybody keep saying that around here? What do they mean everybody knows them? Was I not a part of everybody, because I damn sure don't know him? Shit, I wish I never met him. Just like I wish Rod scary ass wouldn't

have dropped the damn keys. And hold on did this fool just say he was out here

stalking his girl. What the fuck is going on here?

"What should I do?" whispered Rod, timidly.

I didn't even get a chance to answer. "Bruh I just gotta ask yall one

question?" he requested, still looking spooky.

"Wha. Whatsup," asked Rod, hesitantly looking over to the goon.

"Yall seen my girl out hea anywhere?"

"No," Rod replied quickly.

"Your girl?" I asked. Maybe that was the high talking or maybe it was just

my female nosiness but I instantly became curious as to what girl he could be

stalking.

"My bitch. We had a ol petty ass lil bitty argument and she dipped on a

nigga this mornin. "

"So you think she over here?" I asked.

"Yeah. That's her car right there." He said pointing to an older Honda civic,

parked on the street about 20 feet behind us. "She packed all her shit up and I knew

she was gonna be over here."

"So what's the problem?" I asked, loosening my grip on the gun.

"That's the problem," he followed pointing across the street to one of the few cribs without boards on the window "The lights off and her home girl car right there. Her home girl work over nights so she always sleep right around this time. And I can tell the bitch sleep cause all of the lights off."

"Well maybe your girl is sleep too," I followed.

"Yeah," Rod said as he finally reached the keys. He then looked over to me once before inserting the keys into the ignition, then slowly rolled down the car window half way.

"No," Twin shouted. "My girl can't sleep in the dark," he barked aggressively.

"What you mean?" I asked.

"My girl crazy. She gotta have a light on in the house to sleep. That house pitch dark," he said pointing over to the house. "My girl aint in there bruh. My girl aint in there."

"So where you think she at?" I asked.

"She out here fuckin! That's where the hell she at," he shouted.

"No." I said attempting to ease his emotions.

"She may just be riding with her other friends," added Rod.

"My girl aint got no other friends," he looked around. "She riding around with another nigga and he gonna bring her back hea around five in the mornin. I know that cause that's when she gotta go to work. She just parked over hea in case I tried to pop up."

"You might be jumpin to conclusions. She's probably in her friends crib. Chillin." I rebutted.

"Hell naw. I know my girl. I know that bitch. Just come hea right quick. I gotta show yall something," he said motioning for us to follow him.

Rod and I looked over to one another.

"Come on yall. I'm twin. I aint bout to hurt yall."

 Call it a woman's intuition but I trusted Twin. He appeared sincere.

"Come on," I told Rod as we both unsnapped our seatbelts.

I still made sure I took my gun though. I'm not that trusting.

We crept over to the car as Twin placed his right index finger onto his lips motioning for us to be silent.

"Look at that," he said as we arrived. "Look at that."

"What? Lotion"? I asked, peering inside.

"Damn right," he replied as he looked over to us, remembering that he was supposed to be being quiet. "Why is that lotion right there?" he whispered.

"Maybe she was ashy," followed Rod.

"Man hell naw. You see all her bags still in the car," he said as he pointed inside. There were two duffel bags sitting on the back seat. "You mean to tell me she left all her shit in the car and went in her friend crib?"

"Yeah possibly," said Rod.

"Hell naw! Let me tell you what she did," he said before looking around suspiciously. "Let's walk back to yall car."

"What did she do?" asked Rod as we followed.

"Shhh," he said as we made it back over to the car. "Can I sit in the back?"

Rod looked over once more. I signaled yes.

"Yeah," said Rod

We all hopped in. Rod and I focused our attention to Twin. "Let me tell yall what she did. She got hea, called up her lil boyfriend. He picked her up. But before he picked her up. She through on some lotion and left it there. Cause out of everything she packed up. Why is it that the lotion is the only thing left out. Tell me that. That don't make no damn since. I 'ma thinka," he said pointed to his brain. "Trust me. I know my girl."

Rod and I sat quiet.

"Maybe you're jumpin to conclusions though," I said once again.

"No I'm not. I told you I know my girl. This how I met her. She did this to anotha sucka ass nigga. Except I was the one pickin her up back then. She would start a fake ass argument with her nigga so she can come fuck on me all night. I'm tellin you, I know my girl," he said punching his right fist into his left palm. "I know my girl."

"Ok. Ok. That's understandable," said Rod.

"Yeah I guess," I said. So what are you gonna do? Stay out here all night waitin for her?"

"Yep. I tried to call and she keep hangin up. Fuck that. I 'ma wait."

"So if it is another guy, you're not going to beat him up or anything are you?" asked Rod.

"Hell naw it aint his fault."

"Please don't tell me you gonna fight her," I followed.

"Fuck no. I don't hit women. All I'ma say is, Shawty, so you usin me? You usin me Shawty?" said Twin with a serious expression.

"Oh so you think she's usin you?" I asked.

"Yeah. Look at me," he pointed to his designer sweat suit. "I don't work no job. I get money. Real money. I know its bitches out hea who would use me. I just thought shawty was different. That's why I gotta ask her if she usin me. And if she is. Bitch can kick rocks. I just need to know. I'm Twin. Erbody know me. I don't need no bitch."

"You must really love her," said Rod. "I hope she's not doing you like that, bro. You seem like a good dude."

"I am. I aint neva had no girl I love this much. I hope she aint cheatin," he whined, dropping his head in his hands. "But if she is then it's her lost," he followed, gaining his composure. "I'm just mad I wasted so much time on her."

"Yall must've been together for a while," I said sympathetically.

"Yep. Three fucking months."

Rod and I instantly looked at one another. I sat, confused. THREE MONTHS. NIGGA THREE MONTHS? You doing all this for three measly little months. Stalking a bitch after three months. And I was just starting to feel sorry for the guy. But fuck that. I didn't even want to hear anymore. Nigga you better say

fuck that hoe. Are you kidding me? Damn right she's using you. Dumb ass. I

would too. I didn't even want to talk to this clown anymore. I couldn't believe him.

Wasting our damn time.

"Well, Sorry Twin I hope everything works out. But we gotta go," I said,

ending this.

"It's all good shawty. What's yall names anyway?"

"I'm Rod and that's Candy," replied Rod.

"Thanks Rod and Candy. I needed somebody to talk to. Appreciate it," he

said as he opened the car door. "Oh yeah where yall from. Yall don't sound like

yall from around hea."

"Virginia," I said.

"True. So what the hell yall doing in this neighborhood?"

"Had to come see Gucci Mane's old house," Rod said pointing to the

apartments.

"Gucci Mane House? Who told you that was Gucci's crib?" said Twin

confused, chuckling.

"What do you mean," asked Rod.

"You mean to tell me that this isn't the house Gucci grew up in," I asked.

"Hell naw. I don't know who old crib it is but it damn sure aint Gucci," he said laughing. "To tell the truth I don't know where the hell Gucci used to stay. But yall be safe though," he said exiting the vehicle, still laughing.

"Can you believe that shit," I asked Rod in disbelief.

"Drove all the way over here for nothing," replied Rod visibly feeling the same way as I did.

"Just to hear his clown ass cryin about some bitch he knew for 3 months," I followed, placing my gun back in my purse.

"Yeah but look on the bright side, at least we got a good laugh out of it," followed Rod, pulling off.

"Yeah, I guess," I said laughing. "Three fuckin months," I added, shaking my head.

"Yeah. He fucked me up with that. But hey, when you care for someone. I guess there's no time limit on love."

"True, I guess you're right. We only been together for six months but try some dumb shit and best believe your ass is getting stalked too," I said looking and pointing over to him.

"That's cool. I like my girls a little crazy," Rod followed.

We shot back to the hotel, smoked again and took a well needed power nap.

By the time we awoke it was 11:00. I was refreshed and ready to tear the city down. Back home everything closed around two but Atlanta was a whole other story, I'd heard shit was jumping till about 4 or 5 in the morning and I couldn't wait. Who knows? Maybe I'd even run into a couple superstars, after all this was 'Black Hollywood'.

I hopped out the shower to find Rod already dressed, dripping swag from head to toe. All black everything, including his new Robin's. Oh so plain but oh so sexy. First instinct was to throw my wet naked body all over him and I could tell the feeling was mutual as I tip toed over to the clothes I'd left out.

He always bit down on his bottom lip anytime he was ready to make his move and this time was no different. Who could blame him I thought as I walked past a body sized mirror next to the dresser. Body toned, glistening from the Victoria secret lotion I'd just applied before exiting the bathroom.

"Stop right there," I said as Rod attempted to creep over to me.

"What did I do? I just wanted a kiss," replied Rod, stopping in his tracks.

"Nope not until later. We got things to do."

"Yeah, I know, and I'm trying to 'do' them right now," said Rod continuing to walk towards me.

"No," I said pushing him back. "We got plenty of time for all that. We got places to be right now."

"Come on," Rod begged. I just need a little sample to get my night started off right," said Rod as I held him back.

"No. Besides, I have something special planned for us tonight. Just wait on it."

Rod smiled. "Ok I guess. But you better be ready to get nasty later. Real nasty, I got something for that ass," he said, smacking my butt damn near causing a tsunami. "Walking around here looking all good and shit," he followed as he headed to the living room to watch some T.V.

I blushed as I slid on my clothes in front of the mirror. I had gotten the perfect dress made by Luckey, she was known for slaying everyone's dresses in Norview. In my opinion this might be her best creation yet. Remarkable. Let me see, how can I explain it. Ok, I got it, just imagine a sexy red silky robe. Now imagine that it fits my body like a glove, hugging every curve to the T. The right side stops at around my wrist when my arms are down and the left side is raised up like a pair of daisy duke shorts. The arms stop a little before my wrist and my cleavage is poking but not completely. I don't know if you can see it or not but when I tell you I look bomb dot com, please believe it.

Next, I through on my rose gold Michael Kors watch with the blood red face on my left wrist and small rose gold tennis bracelet on my right, which went perfect along with my rose gold choker. To top it off I killed the game with my first pair of Christian Louboutin Red Bottom 6 inch pumps, all black with the red on the bottom. Oh yeah I can't forget my Yves Saint Laurent 'Opium' perfume. Gosh Almighty! Can the church say Amen! It's gotta be a sin to look this good. Damn.

I stared in the mirror applying my makeup. Nothing major, just a little eye shadow and a dab of red lipstick. Rod better be lucky I aint no hoe because as I studied myself from top to bottom I'm all but positive I could pull me a baller tonight. But shit, as good as he looking I'm pretty sure he could bag any girl he pleased too. Together, Facebook and Instagram was about to get shut the fuck down! Do you hear me?

After taking a gazillion pictures it was time to pregame. We both popped our molly. This was by far the first time. We'd grown to love the drug over the last couple months. In my opinion it's like the best drug ever created. It seems to bring out feelings and emotions inside of you that sometimes can't be tapped into without it. It's like we can talk about anything. And the sex! Ah man the sex is absolutely amazing. Imagine having sex on a cloud, with the person of your dreams, right after you win the lotto. Now multiply that by ten! Yep, that's how good it is. It's a struggle not doing it every day. But the thought of becoming Pookie and the prom Queen from New jack city keeps us from going too far. But trust me it's the shit.

Yeah, so we popped the molly took a couple shots of Remi 1738 in honor of one of our other favorite rappers, Fetty Wap and headed out the door. By now it was 1 in the morning. Ignoring the fact that it was dark out, I through on my Versace shades and headed out. Make room, A superstar is coming through I thought as I floated through the lobby.

The night was beautiful. The beginning of winter, yet only 50 degrees and with the molly and liquor in my system it felt even warmer. I rested in Rods arms as we awaited the arrival of the valet.

Not long after, we hopped in, I leaned my seat back, vibing to the Gangster sounds of Boosie BadAzz.

We arrived at the club around 1:30. Still, as late as it was, the line was still wrapped around the corner. Thank God we made it on time. Turns out we were going to be the last two to get in.

After about 20 minutes we'd finally arrived to the front of the line. Then it hit me. Fuck! We'd forgotten one crucial piece of info. We were only 18, trying to get into a 21 and up club.

"Sorry, 21 and up. No exceptions," said the security, some big black cock diesel nigga, as Rod flashed him his worthless I.D.

"Aw man come on. We're from outta town we came all the way up here from Virginia to come to your club. You mean to tell me we can't get in?" I followed. I'd sweet talked my way out of plenty situations. Hopefully this would be one.

"Yeah that's exactly what I mean," he said looking around, never in my eyes as if I wasn't important. Still I wasn't about to give up.

"So you telling me there's no way I can get in?" I asked.

"Nope," he said quickly. "Come on. You know I don't make the rules. That's just how it is. It's plenty of clubs in The 'A' that will let you in but we just can't do it here. Sorry, I don't know what more to tell you."

"What about for this?" Rod chimed in sliding a little cash into his hands.

The bouncer peeked into his hands to see what Rod had given him. He mouthed the words '$20'. "Nigga if you don't take this bullshit back, I can't even put gas in my Hummer with that. Yall mite needa go on back home. This town a little too grown for yall," he said attempting to return Rods money. I then reached into my purse, sliding him two crisp $100 bills.

"How about now?" I asked

He peeked inside his hand before looking over to Rod. "See, you better keep this one right here. She know a little somethin. This Atlanta, you gotta pay to play around here," he then opened the little red velvet gate thing and put his arm out leading us into the club.

"Thanks." I said.

"No problem. I already know that you know not to say anything?" he asked making sure I was hip to the no snitching policy.

"About what?" I followed as we walked in.

"Yeah my nigga. You definitely gotta keep her," he said smiling.

"I already know," followed Rod.

As luck would have it, there was no one on the inside to take our money for the cover price. So we slid on through.

I walked in slowly making sure I took in everything around me. My eyes transformed into cameras as I mentally took snapshots of my surroundings. This experience was definitely one to remember. The place was packed. Wall to wall

action. First thing I noticed as I entered was the bar full of top shelf liquor,

surrounded by shot callers and the women they desired, toasting to the good life.

To the right or the bar was a huge stage along with three poles attached, where

women of all nationalities with Coke bottle bodies' twerked poetically to the

sounds of 'Korb Skii'. Some on stage and some sliding magically down the three

poles they had set up. Gotta admit I felt a little out of place. Never had I been in a

room and didn't feel like I was the baddest but this night was different. I clutched

on to Rod's hand as I looked around observing countless other butt naked beauties

simulating sex on different men's laps throughout the club. The aroma of

California Marijuana filled the room overpowering any other smells, causing a

mist like cloud upon us.

Scattered throughout were a few women like myself, either twerking on the

dance floor or sitting down next to their girlfriends or man.

"Baby Look," said Rod as he pointed.

"What?"

"Look who's here," Rod said directing my attention to what looked like a

V.I.P. section on the far end of the club.

"Oh shit is that who I think it is?" I asked, squinting my eyes to get a better look.

"Yep. Korb Skii," replied Rod over the blaring music.

"Oh shit," this definitely is the place to be. Korb Skii was a rapper from VA. He'd recently hit big and I must admit, it felt good to see him make it. Everyone in town had personally watched him grind for years. Although he wasn't from Norview, he'd always come through and perform at our little clubs. He's from Norfolk, that's about an hour or two away from Norview. I never mentioned it to Rod but I was told Skii had wanted my number at one point. Too bad Chop found out and cut all that short. I wonder what life would have been like with a famous rapper. He always seemed like a really nice guy. But what do I know, that probably would all have changed after he got famous. I know how that lifestyle can get. I guess I'll just be happy with what I have. And as I looked over to Rod that most definitely wasn't a bad thing.

We walked over to the bar.

"Is this where we come to get ones?" asked Rod.

"Yes," followed the bartender. Damn, even she was bad. Looked sort of like a Smooth Magazine model. Her large caramel breast sat perky in a red leather halter top while her round plump ass sported black booty shorts that struggled to hold all that she had to offer. She wasn't quite as cute as me but I still inched closer to Rod "What you workin with?" she asked.

Rod looked over to me, he had a couple hundred but I held most of the money in my purse. I pulled out 5 one hundred dollar bills and handed them all to the girl. Yeah I know five hundred was a lot but compared to the blizzard of bills I watched Korb Skii and his crew throw, I felt I had too. Besides, trust and believe we were gonna make that shit last all night. Who knows, we might even go home with some. Usually Rod is the cheap one but I'm still not all the way sure how I feel about giving some bitch all my money.

We ordered two double shots of Remy on the rocks and copped a squat in two chairs next to the stage.

Rod was entranced by the butt naked hoes. It was written all over his face.

"Baby," said rod as he looked over to me, eyes half closed sporting a jokers grin.

"Whatsup," I asked looking over to him.

"I feel it,"

"Feel what?"

"The molly," he said smiling harder. "It just kicked in."

At that moment mine started marching through my body like a HBCU Drum Major on Homecoming day. "Me too," I said. I immediately began grinding my teeth as the 'Heavenly' feel took over. While most people say it takes their appetite. Instead I go through the polar opposite. I became famished and as I continued looking around I peeped niggas throwing back chicken wings. I'd always heard strip club chefs were the best. It was a must that I tried some.

"I'll be right back baby."

"Where are you going?" asked Rod as I interrupted him from staring at the countless women.

"I'm starvin. Gotta order some wings," I said.

"Hold on isn't one of the waitresses going to come around and ask?"

"Probably but I need some now," I replied, standing to my feet. I don't got time to wait."

"Ok, can you get me some too?" he asked as he looked back over to the bitches.

"Yeah," I said as I walked away, attempting to remain focused.

"Hot. Real hot," I heard Rod scream.

"Ok," I shouted, still never looking back as I made my way over to the bar. "Hey. Is this where I order the wing?" I asked the girl who'd given us the ones.

"It sure is," said the woman before looking up. She smiled when she noticed it was me. "What flavor and how many would you like?" she asked.

I smiled back. "I don't know, shit, hundred, I'm hungry as a motherfucker."

"Ok. Well you know wings aint the only thing we got to eat around here," she said as she rested her arms on the bar bringing her doll like face closer to me, licking her already moist lips. If I didn't know any better I'd think she was flirting with me.

"What else good you have to eat?" I asked flirtatiously. I'd never done this before. I always said I would never have a threesome but who knows. Maybe it would be fun. Plus I did tell Rod that I had something special for him. To be honest I didn't have a damn thing planned. I just said that shit just to be saying it. But this bitch right here was making me think. I just didn't know how to approach her. It wasn't every day a bad bitch was tryna get a slice of my pie. Sure the ugly, fishy ass, butch dykes in Norview were always shooting their shots but eww I'd never take them serious. How could I?

"I got somethin warm and juicy for you," she replied.

"Oh really," I said as we locked eyes. I think I had her right where I wanted her.

Suddenly she took her eyes from me. "Is that your boyfriend over there?" she pointed.

"Uh huh," I said smiling, eyes still focused on her. She must've saw Rod and couldn't wait to get this threesome popping. Shit why wouldn't she. I mean Rod didn't have on a lick of jewelry but as far as sex appeal he was still holding his own in a room full of money.

"Well, I think he's in a little bit of trouble," she followed.

"Trouble?" I asked before realizing what she'd just said. "Trouble!" I shouted as I discovered about three overgrown security niggas posted up around Rod as some stripper disapprovingly pointed her index finger at him.

I hopped away from the bar tender, sprinting my way over. Forgetting I had on heels, I fell, busting my ass on the floor. Before I could get up some nigga tried to assist me. "You alright," he said as he grabbed my hand pulling me up. "What your fine ass doin in hea? I know you can't work hea."

"Nigga shut the fuck up," I replied as I snatched my hand before pushing him away from me, making my way back to my man. "What the fuck are yall doin?" I screamed as I finally made it. By now two security guards were on both sides of Rod dragging him away as onlookers stared.

"Yo get the fuck off of him," I screamed once again, pushing the one to the right to no avail. No matter how much molly I had in my system dude was just too big, he was like a Refrigerator or something

"Chill baby. It's cool," followed Rod as they continued carrying him away.

"Naw fuck that. We paid good money to get in here. Get off of him." I said pushing him once more.

"Get your girl dog," said the security, still trotting away.

"Baby just chill. Everything's ok," screamed Rod.

Fuck that I immediately begin throwing haymakers before another security came from nowhere, picking me up. "Get the fuck off me," I yelled swinging irately, trying my absolute hardest to remove myself from his grasp.

"Yeah get the fuck off of her," followed Rod vigorously attempting to break loose from the other security's grasp. He had no luck either as they scooped him up. Now we both traveled, feet in the air, dangling, before they tossed us out onto the winter concrete, Jazzy Jeff style. I hopped up, adjusting my dress, attempting to mentally block out the cars riding passed honking in amusement. So fucking embarrassing.

"AAHHHH," I screamed, sprinting to the club door before it was abruptly slammed in my face. "What the fuck," I shouted, storming off. "I got something for they ass."

"Baby what are you doing?" asked Rod, following behind me.

"I'm gonna go get the strap out the car. I'm about to shoot this bitch up. Fuck that. Who the fuck they think they are? Kicking us out for no damn reason after we paid $200 to get in that wack ass club."

"Baby. Chill," said Rod, now running to catch up to me. "Baby you're not going to shoot the damn club up. Fuck it. We can go to a better club tomorrow," he stated as he began running out of breath.

Ok, Rod was right. I wasn't about to shoot shit up. I just heard Chop say it so much back in the day I guess I thought that was what you were supposed to say. But I definitely needed to let off some steam. I was livid, wishing I knew where those bitch ass niggas parked, I'd flatten all their tires and bust every window they got. They must aint know they was fucking with the Princess of Norview. Somebody better tell them.

I screamed once more before Rod grabbed me by the shoulder. "Baby its ok."

"You think its ok for someone to just kick us out for no damn reason after we paid all that money? It must be some kinda scam they got to get extra dough," I said, shoving him away from me, before drunkenly screaming "Bitches!" towards the club ignoring the fact that no one could hear me.

"I actually did sort've do something."

"Huh. What? What the hell did you do?" I asked, turning to him so that we were face to face.

"It's not really what did I do. It's more like what happened," Rod explained.

"Ok. So what the fuck happened Trevor. What could you possibly have done to get us kicked the fuck out?" I asked as Rod stood, fiddling his fingers, head down like a kindergartener telling his mom what he had done to get in time out in school that day.

"My dick slipped out," Rod mumbled, still not raising his head.

"What? What are you talkin about?"

"My dick slipped out these fake ass Robin Jeans," he said as he pointed down to his broken zipper.

"Hold on. Explain," I said taking a deep breath.

"Ok," said Rod, finally lifting his head. "So when you walked away to get the chicken. One of the dancers walked over to me and asked if I wanted a dance. I said sure why not. So, she starts dancing on me and what not and as she sat on my lap she hopped up and ran. I looked down and my dick was sticking out of my pants."

I organized my thoughts before speaking. This had to be a joke "So you mean to tell me your dick got so hard off that nasty ass bitch that your damn dick burst through your drawls and broke your zipper?" I asked combatively. "Huh? Is that what you're tryna to tell me?"

"No. Hell no. Let me explain. I have on boxers, my dick slips out the little whole all the time," Rod, explained, slowly. "But this time with my zipper being broke I guess it just came all the way out. I don't know."

"You don't fuckin know? Man you fuckin dumb," I shouted, walking away.

"I'm dumb? You're the one who wanted to listen to Westside P. He's the one you should be mad at," replied Rod, following me. "He sold us the busted jeans and sent us to the wrong damn house. Not me."

"No," I shouted, never looking back. "What does he have to do with this? Aint nobody tell your ol fast ass to get a lap dance soon as I get up. I bet you couldn't wait for me to leave. You probably wanted some alone time with your lil stripper bitch," I ranted as I turned around for a quick second to ensure he could see my anger.

"Huh? Are you serious? I never even told you to leave. You left on your own. I'm the one who told you a waitress was on her way. Remember?"

"Whatever," I said continuing my path. "Fuckin Pervert."

"I'm not a pervert," Rod shouted frantically trying to catch up with me once again.

"Whatever. Just open up the door," I said as I reached the car. I stood, arms folded.

We got into the car. "So what you want to do now?" asked Rod.

"Just take me to the fuckin hotel," I shouted, pouting.

"You know you don't really want to go to the hotel. Where do you want to go Candy?" he asked looking over to me, eyes still low.

I sat silent ignoring him arms still folded. He was right I didn't want to go to the hotel. The molly was in my system and I couldn't imagine being caged in some little ass hotel room. The drug usually amplifies whatever mood you're in. So that should give you a little clue on how I'm feeling right now."

"I'm sorry baby."

"It's ok. You're a perv. You were born like that, you can't help it," I said calmly. "Your dad and all your Uncles were probably pervs, who knows," I said looking straight ahead.

"Chill baby. I'm not a perv. I just explained to you what went down. What can I say, shit happens."

"Yeah, yeah. Let's just go to the room. I'm tired of bein over here. I don't want to be reminded of what just happened for another second."

By now Rod was searching through his phone. "Baby I think I found another club we can go to. It's only about 5 minutes away. You want to go?"

I ignored him. Yeah I wanted to go but I wanted him to feel my anger a little more first.

"Baby. You want to go. Huh?" he asked sweetly.

"I don't know. I'm a little scared. I don't want to get thrown out onto the cold ass concrete again. Aint like you gonna do somethin to the security."

"What was I supposed to do?"

"I don't know. All I know is if I was a man and some big ass nigga through my girl out the club I'd be a lil more angry."

"What do you want me to do?" asked Rod. "What? You want me to go shoot up the club or something?"

"Nope I don't want you to do a thing."

"Damn baby. Stop acting like that. I said I'm sorry."

"Ok. I heard you. Are we going to this other club or not. I told you I'm tired of sittin here," I asked still never making eye contact.

"You never even told me if you wanted to go or not."

"Oh my God. Just be the man and take over sometimes. Damn. Why am I always callin the shots?" I asked, finally looking over to him.

"Here we go again. I'm always a bitch anytime you get mad."

"Bitch? I never said that. You must think that about yourself. Sorry you feel that way."

"See, usually when you say shit like that I get mad. But not tonight. I'm not going to let it ruin our night. I'm going to take your advice. And take charge."

"Whatever," I said as Rod pulled off.

We arrived at 'Phatz' around 3:00. It was some little hole in the wall strip club, they didn't even ask for I.D.'s and there was no line to get in as I strolled in behind Rod, arms still crossed as the smell of cigarettes, booty, and cheap alcohol smacked me dead in my face. I looked around at the talent, beer bellies, cellulite, knotty tracks and poorly done make up was obviously a qualification when applying.

"What do you think?" asked Rod over the loud music. They were playing Korb Skii's 'Last Night'. Too bad he'd never step foot in this place. I wonder if they knew he was down the street at a real strip club.

"Think about what?" I asked, arms still crossed.

"The club. Yeah I know it's not like the last one but we always got tomorrow. "I didn't speak. "Let's just sit down," Rod said pointing to a small round table next to us. "I'm going to go get us something to drink and some wings."

I examined my seat for rodents before cautiously sitting down as Rod trotted off. Never the one to act boogie but I had no choice but to turn my nose up at these hoes. Ew, disgusting. I was probably the baddest bitch who'd ever stepped foot in this dump. Not just judging from the strippers but because I was the only female besides a group of fat bitches to the left of me, with clothes on.

And worse of all these strippers couldn't even twerk. Booty's looking all hard and stiff. Who agreed to hire these hoes? I need to see management. Hell is going on around here. But shit I guess broke niggas who can only afford to throw a dollar or two still needed somewhere to go. Still, yuck, I scanned the room attempting to find something worth throwing some cash at.

All I thought as I looked around was, too fat, too skinny, eww, still got hair on her coochie, too tall, feet too long and her toes aint done, then I found her, like a needle in a haystack. Of course she was already staring at me. She wasn't on stage with the other booger bears. Instead, she was on the floor butt naked giving some fat nigga a lap dance. Still, as she twerked, booty to his face, her eyes were locked on me. Don't forget the molly was still in me causing me to feel as if we were the only two in the room. Naturally she said fuck the Pillsbury dough boy and strolled her way over to me. I studied her body as she came closer. She appeared to be about my size, nice tits and from what I could see, her face was ok, brown skin, her weave wasn't all that expensive but it wasn't nearly as cheap looking as some of the others.

"Hey Sexy," she leaned over and whispered to me as I noticed her teeth were straight, well at least the ones I could see. The entire bottom row were covered with gold and something that looked like diamonds.

I remained silent, gazing into her hazel eyes as I gently bit down on the right corner of my lip.

"I know you not in hea by yourself," she asked seductively southern as she grinded her body to the beat.

"Nope, I'm with my man," I replied as I nodded my head over to Rod. He was still at the bar. I decided to try my luck. Truth be told I wasn't really that mad that Rod had gotten us kicked out the club anymore and if I was really gonna go through with this threesome plan I might as well choose this bitch.

"Him over there in the all black?" she asked, continuing to dance as we both looked over to Rod who wasn't paying us any mind.

"Yep. You like him?" Boy, why the fuck did I ask her that shit? Knowing damn well I'm not prepared for the answer. Look at me, always going in over my head. I said a small prayer before she could answer. 'Lord Please don't let me beat this bitch ass if she give me the wrong answer.'

"Yeah, yall look good togetha," she replied.

Ok. Ok. I can deal with that. I don't see a reason to mop her ass up. Thank God!

"We'll look even better with you," I said as she proceeded to give me a lap dance. It may sound disgusting but I sniffed the air as she danced, making sure I didn't smell anything unusual. She was good though.

At that moment I realized I hadn't thrown a single dollar her way. I then reached in my purse, grabbing a wad before tossing it up in the air.

"I was just thinkin the same thing," She said as she sat forward in my lap, whispering in my ear. "Where yall going after this?"

"Our hotel. We're not from around here," I whispered back.

"Even better," she moaned as she eased her way off my lap. "Put my numba in your phone" she said turning around to face me. I pulled out my jack as she inched closer to me. "4043342345," she said as I typed it into my phone. "I'm bouta cash out in ten minutes, we got a shower and everything back there. I can call you as soon as I'm on my way."

"Perfect," I said looking over to Rod who was now walking back with two drinks in hand. "Actually make sure you text me," I said as I sent her a text 'Candy'.

She nodded and walked to the back. I'd told her to text first because I wanted this to be a surprise for Rod.

"You see anything you like?" asked Rod as he finally arrived back oblivious as to what had just occurred.

"Not really," I replied looking around.

"Damn baby. I'm sorry." Rod said appearing sad.

"It's ok. You were right. We always have tomorrow," I followed attempting to cheer him up.

"So you ready to go?"

"That depends. Did you order some hot wings?"

"Yeah there gonna be up soon."

"Well just let me get my wings and then we can be out. Trust me you're not gonna regret it when we get to the telly," I said with a flirtatious smirk.

"I bet. So you don't want to throw anything at the strippers?" he asked as we both scanned once more with our noses turned up.

"No baby. But you can." I handed him a bankroll. "Have fun. I'll be over here sitting pretty, something these bitches know nothing about," I said as I crossed my legs.

"You damn sure right about that," followed Rod as he looked around before making his way to the stage.

"Hey baby," I shouted as Rod turned around. "Keep your dick in your paints." He chuckled before continuing his path.

He sipped his drink next to the stage where three of the ratchet bitches tried their absolute hardest to win every dime from him. But due to the fact my man was the opposite of these bitches pussies; tight, and the fact that I've sent him countess videos of me shaking my ass thousands of times better than them, them bitches barely made $20 off of him.

By the time my wings arrived Rod was back.

"Baby, I've got to tell you one more time. I'm sorry for getting us kicked out. I never want to come here again. Do you smell that?" he sniffed.

"Yes," I replied.

As the night went on the unpleasant odor of unkempt pussy had grown stronger. We quickly decided it would be better to get a to go box and eat on the way.

I turned on some Jodeci as we drove home. I could tell he was feeling it so I turned things up a notch, through my leg up on the dash, wearing no underwear, I pleasured myself before grabbing his hand to showcase how wet I'd become. Angelica was in full force.

"Baby can we pull over?" he asked.

I shook my head slow as I sucked the juices from my fingertips.

"Girl, you don't know what I'm going to do to you," he shouted, as he reached over soaking his fingertips in my juices once again. Only, I smacked his hand away this time. I remained in full control.

We rushed back into the room. I made sure I walked in front of him to assure he had a clear view of my ass wobbling and bouncing as I stepped. Before I could get to the room I received a text.

'Hey, it's Tasty, What's the address baby?' I quickly sent it to her and in no time she texted back. "Cool. I can be there in 20 minutes."

I smiled as I opened the room door.

"I'm gonna take a shower. You wait right here," I said.

"You sure we can't take one together. I don't bite," followed Rod as he caressed my ass.

I smiled, again not speaking as I made my way to the bathroom closing the door, turning on the lights and stripping down to my birthday suit before hopping in. I scrubbed my body and thanks to the Molly I was undoubtedly loving the feeling of my touch, causing me to slightly forget that 'Tasty' was on her way.

"Baby, you ok in there?" shouted Rod as he knocked on the door forcing me to suddenly remember what I was doing.

"Yeah, I'm comin right out," I replied as I cut off the water, hopped out and through on my towel. "Your turn," I said as I walked out still dripping wet in more ways than one.

"Damn, you look good," said Rod as he grabbed his already hard dick. "Be ready when I come out. You think you got something for me but you haven't seen nothing yet," he said as he entered the bathroom.

I smiled as he shut the door. Went over to my phone. I had a text. "I'm here. What's the room number?"

I text back and got everything set up. Through on my freaky deaky playlist, equipped with certified baby makers, Chris Brown, R. Kelly and just about any other slow jam classic you can imagine. I then lit a few candles, pulled out my handcuffs and blindfold out my bag and awaited Tasty patiently.

It wasn't long before I received the text I was looking for. 'I'm at the door'. I walked through the living room, still in my towel. I was gonna throw on some lingerie but if I know Rod like I think I do than I know he'd rather me be naked.

I opened my door. There she was. Still Pretty. Believe it or not, even prettier in the light. Everything on her was on point, face and body. And as she slid past me into the room I noticed Shorty was packing back there. How had I missed that bubble butt in the club? It appeared to be real but due to the fact that we were in Atlanta I couldn't tell. I guess I'll find out sooner or later.

I shut the door leading to the living room and gave Tasty the instructions as we waited for the sound of the water to cease.

"Baby I'm coming out Butt ass naked. Don't get scared now!" shouted Rod.

"Ok baby," I said as I walked over to the entrance of the bathroom.

I stopped him in his tracks as he attempted to walk out. "Hold on baby. Put this on," I said as I handed him the blindfold."

"Aw shit," he said as he wrapped it around his eyes. I gawked at his body. Good lord. I took a deep breath and thought long and hard on if I could actually share this. Guess it's too late now though.

"Can you see?"

"No," Rod replied, smiling.

"You, sure?" I asked as I jumped at him. He didn't flinch.

"Baby, I promise. I'm ready. Let's get this show on the road."

I grabbed his hand as I escorted him over to the bed, sitting him down at the edge. I then moved over to the side as Tasty crept in front of him, dropping massage oil over his body. "Oh shit," he said.

"Shhhh," said Tasty as she pushed him back onto the bed, sliding her hands up and down his chiseled naked body.

"Baby," he moaned before she slowly dragged her hands from his shoulders down to his manhood. He'd grown so aroused that his dick began jumping up and down uncontrollably before she could even get a chance to wrap her luscious lips around it.

Finally, thrusted open his legs, hopping between before sucking and massaging his long throbbing penis simultaneously.

After a minute or two, it was now time for me to tap in. Climbing carefully onto the bed I eased my way over top of him, dropping my coochie onto his face as we faced opposite directions, I slowly ran my fingers through Tasty's hair as she relentlessly deep throated. "Oh my God," I heard him say as we both moaned in ecstasy.

This wasn't too bad. Slow and sensual, just like I liked it, my pussy juices flooded his face as he pleasured every spot I desired. His stiff tongue wandered knowingly around my clit, slow then fast, discovering land I never knew existed. My eyes rolled so far back in my head I'm surprised they didn't get lost. Unable to control myself I removed my hands from Tasty's head, gripping the bed sheets as my toes through up gang signs while my legs uncontrollably jerked knocking pillows to the floor. I called out 'Rod', as I closed my eyes releasing everything my body stored inside of me.

Snapping back into reality, everything changed. Devilish anger consumed me as I discovered this bitch hopping up and down on my man's dick, cow girl style as she covered him in her stripper juices. Booty bouncing, she moaning, his bitch as even stopped licking me to utter "Oh Shit," as his teeth chattered.

"Oh hell naw," I screamed as I violently hopped up swinging, handing out lightning fast jabs.

"Baby, what the fuck are you doing?" bellowed Rod as he took the blindfold off, attempting to break up the one sided fight.

"Get off me," screamed Tasty as I knocked her to the ground.

"Chill baby," followed Rod as he attempted to hold me back. "OUCH," rod screamed, releasing me after I viciously bit a chunk from his arm.

"Bitch you gettin the fuck out here," I said as I dragged Tasty by her hair, while opening the living room door before tossing her naked ass out the main door, slamming it shut, as she continued screaming.

"What the fuck is your problem?" yelled Rod.

Tasty banged on the door, screaming and shouting, "Bitch I'ma kill you."

"Fuck you bitch," I barked back, ignoring Rod.

"Yo, I said what the fuck is your problem?" bellowed Rod as I picked up Tasty's cheap ass clothes.

"Bitch, stop bangin on my damn door," I screamed as I opened the door, throwing her clothes to her.

"Ok. Ok. Bitch you got it. You got it," screamed Tasty as she stomped down the hall.

"Do you hear me?" asked Rod. He had followed me into the living room.

"Fuck you!"

"What I do?

"So you just gon fuck that bitch right in front of me," I shouted, furiously.

"What? It was your fucking idea. Are you crazy?"

"Naw bitch, are you crazy. I never once told you to fuck that bitch. Walkin around here with her stinking ass cum all on your dick," I said pointing to his now limp penis.

"You never told me anything. It was a surprise, remember," said Rod as I rapidly searched for a blanket.

"Nigga, I aint tryna hear that shit. And got the nerve to fuck her without a condom. I can't believe you."

"To be honest I didn't know who I was fucking or eating. I was just going with the flow. How was I supposed to know?" asked Rod as he shadowed me.

"What?" I screamed. "So you mean to tell me you ate my pussy like that and didn't even know it was me? Fuck you!" I screamed one more time.

"Fuck me. No bitch fuck you," shouted Rod.

"Bitch?" I yelled as I rushed him throwing my fist at his face. Too bad I was too short. He dodged every blow before grabbing me.

"You better calm down!"

"Fuck you, get the fuck off me," I screamed as Rod released me. "I hate you," I said as I found some extra covers in the closet by the front door. "Get the fuck out here," I said pointing to the room as I flopped down on the couch, throwing the cover over my head. I was livid.

"Fucking crazy," Rod mumbled.

"Naw bitch, that's your Daddy," I yelled.

"What?" screamed Rod.

No reply, grinded my teeth, still high off the molly, I drifted off until the world faded away.

I awoke the next afternoon, half way sober, looking for the mess I'd made. There was none. Had this been a dream? Nope. Figured that out as I saw Rod walk out the bedroom, fully dressed in a hoody and jeans. He looked over to me in disappointment. I thought about saying sorry, but I had to think about it. Yeah, I was the one who arranged the threesome but how could he not know which girl was me. And if he see me beating this bitch ass why was he trying to break it up. Yeah, like I said fuck him.

"You hungry?" he asked without looking over to me. "The wings from last night fell on the floor during the fight. I had to throw them away."

I wanted to say no until I suddenly felt a grizzly bear growling inside of me. "Yeah, I don't care."

"Alright get dressed. We can find something I guess."

I slowly got up, took another shower, brushed my teeth, and through on a comfy black 'Pink' sweat suit and my smoke Gray Uggs. Thank God, I have these braids in my hair, because I'd hate to have to style it.

We made our way to the lobby, the both of us on our phones, ignoring one another. Remembering I'd left my purse with the money and gun in the room I quickly thought 'forget it', Rod had the key and I definitely wasn't in the mood to ask him for anything.

Rod told the valet to bring our car before we headed outside to await him. About a minute of uncomfortable silence went by, when suddenly ten of the ratchet strippers from 'Phatz' along with some guy suddenly rushed towards us. "That's that bitch right there," screamed Tasty.

I started to run, only problem was my feet seemed to be sticking to the concrete. In no time they'd surrounded me, punching and kicking as I ducked my head swinging recklessly as they connected with my face and body, pulling my hair in all types of directions. I struggled to stand as I noticed less and less hands attacking me.

As I slowly raised my head I discovered every single one of the bitches were on the ground and Rod was dealing out a killer jab to the one guy as he too dropped. "Fuck wrong with yall?" yelled Rod as veins seemed to be nearly bursting out of his body.

At the same time valet pulled up. "Baby, get in," said Rod as I rushed to the passenger seat, still in shock.

"We gon kill yall, Yall dead," screamed some of the stripper bitches as they gathered each other up.

"What's going on out here?" asked the hotel workers as they rushed out on their walky talkies.

Too late. Rod peeled off.

"What just happen," I asked as I looked in the mirror, examining my face.

"We just beat some fucking ass. That's what the fuck just happen," boasted Rod.

"Oh my God, they pulled a braid out I said as I looked at my head." Not only had they pulled a braid but my nose was leaking. "And look at my nose," I said before I quickly stuffed a napkin inside my nostril. Still, I guess I couldn't be too mad, nothing else was wrong besides the throbbing headache I'd just obtained.

"Fuck that bae. You're good. Still beautiful," Rod said looking over to me. He was looking like a straight up G. I had never seen him like this. I can tell his adrenaline was pumping as his chest puffed in and out while he breathed like a fat kid after chasing the ice cream truck for too long.

"Baby. You really just had my back," I said in awe.

"What? Candy, I'd kill for you," he replied as he stared in my eyes. "Long as I'm around nobody and I mean nobody's going to hurt you," he said as he pulled up to a red light.

I smiled, speechless as I leaned over to give him a kiss.

BOW. BOW. BOW. Gunshots rang out and glass shattered as I screamed in terror while Rod quickly stepped on the gas. These bitches were dumping on us. I held on tightly to my seat frantically panicking as Rod maneuvered in and out of traffic as the thots tailed us, still shooting. I heard the back window seem to explode as Rod sped through a red light.

BOOM! The sound of cars colliding shot through my ears. I looked back and the bitches had caused a three car accident as Rod glided onto the interstate ramp. God must've been on our side because I'm positive Rod had no idea where we were going.

"Oh my God. Oh my God. Oh my God. Oh my God," I screamed as I struggled to get myself together.

Rod remained silent, focused as we zoomed down the highway, bumping Gucci Mane's 'East Atlanta 6' before escaping onto the nearest exit ramp.

"You ok, baby," he finally asked as he seemingly snapped back into reality.

"Yes, yes, Oh my God! Are you? Are you ok?" I asked, distraught.

"I'm good baby. Those bitches can't see us!" Rod shouted in triumph as we pulled into a Wendy's, parking lot to regroup.

Not wasting a second, Rod hopped out the whip to check things out. Still in shock, I couldn't quite move. But just watching him as he searched around the whip made me realize just how fucking dumb I was. I snap on him, call him bitches, soft, for absolutely no good reason. I now realize why I always thought he wasn't a real man. I had never actually knew one. My Dad's been M.I.A. since I can remember and Chop did me dirty, actually beyond dirty, still I acted as though Rod was less of a man because he didn't act like him. Chop isn't a man. But Trevor Alexander Smith is and has been one since the first day I laid eyes on him. Probably one of the greatest to ever walk the earth. God had purposely sculpted him just for me. No matter how I treat him he always has my back like no other. A tear fell from my eyes as I'd finally understood what I had in my possession all this time. A rider. A real true love, something bitches would kill for. And here I was basically tearing us down every chance I could get, when he's truly all I have and all I've wanted. Am I retarded or what?

"We good, aint no tires busted," said Rod as he sat down in the driver's seat. "Just the two windows busted out. We can get that shit fixed today. No problem. We good. Them hoes can't shoot. We supposed to have been dead," he said before looking over to me. "What you crying for baby? It's ok. I told you we good."

"It's not that," I said looking back at him.

"What it is?"

"I love you. I really fuckin love you."

"You love me?" Rod asked bashfully. "You've never told me that before."

"I know. And I'm sorry. I've known for a while actually," I followed, sincerely.

A tear fell from Rods right eye. "I love you too Candy. More than anything."

We leaned over for a classic kiss. Despite what had just occurred. This was undoubtedly the greatest moment of my life, hands down. Candy and Rod vs. the World.

If you enjoyed Us vs. Them make sure you spread the word.

If you purchased on Amazon or Kindle please leave a review.

If you're incarcerated please request to get this book and my other novels 'American Rap Star', 'American Maniac, 'American Boy', and my latest, 'American Dream', in the building!

Thank you for the support. If you need to contact me:
Phone: 757-708-4890
Facebook: Kevin Brown
Instagram: __KevinBrown
Website:KevinBrownBooks.com

Made in the USA
Middletown, DE
12 February 2022

60864349R00066